Trojan Rooster

Stories by Quan Zhang

DIXIE W PUBLISHING CORPORATION U.S.A.
美国南方出版社

Published by Dixie W Publishing Corporation
Montgomery, Alabama, U.S.A.
http://www.dixiewpublishing.com

Copyright © 2019 by Quan Zhang

All rights reserved.
No part of this book may be reproduced in any form or by any electronic or mechanical means including information storage and retrieval systems, without permission in writing from the publisher. The only exception is by a reviewer, who may quote short excerpts in a review.

Printed in the United States of America
9 8 7 6 5 4 3 2 1
First Printing: October 2019

Library of Congress Control Number: 2019949705
ISBN-13: 978-1-68372-211-3

for Peggy

Also by Quan Zhang

Wisteria Arbor

Generation Mao: a memoir

Speaking Up

Expatriates

CONTENTS

Introduction 1

Trojan Rooster 10
Chicken Blood Therapy 26
Colonel Ma's Father 42
The Birds & Bees In Beijing 58
The Bridge 69
The Balcony 87
The Jaundice Ward 97
Chimeras 118
Flight 144
Inspection 164
Defection 179
Boomerang 200

About The Author 247

Introduction

In May 1995, we arrived in Seattle. Soon after our arrival, we walked into a store called Bulldog News near the University of Washington. In the literary journal section, I stumbled upon an English short story written

by a Chinese writer with the pen name Ha Jin. I was intrigued.

Ha Jin was born in 1956 in Liaoning Province, China. He received his B.A. in English from Heilongjiang University in 1981 and his M.A. in American Literature in 1984 from Shandong University. After earning a PhD in literature from the University of Brandeis in the United States in

1992, he engaged in creative writing in English. At the time, Ha Jin was not well-known, but the story he'd written for an English language literary journal as well as our similar backgrounds inspired me to try creative writing in English.

The first story I wrote in English, titled "Colonel Ma's Father," was accepted by the Department of Literature, American University, on November 7, 1995, and was published in the 1996 winter issue of Folio: **A literary Journal**. [1]

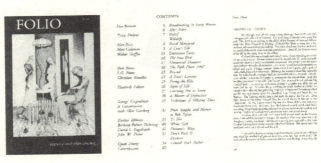

After writing "Colonel Ma's Father," I went on to write the second story titled "The balcony."[2]

---

[1] "Colonel Ma's Father," the Winter 1996 issue of Folio: A literary Journal

[2] "The Balcony," the 13th Anniversary 1996 (Vol.30 Nos. 2-3) issue of Wisconsin Review

I tried to use the stream of consciousness and disrupted time sequence that William Faulkner had used so well in his novel, <u>The Sound and the Fury</u>. As in Faulkner's novel, the protagonist is mentally challenged. From his place of imprisonment on the balcony of his family's apartment, in a privileged residential compound, he watches the unfolding of some of the madness of the Cultural Revolution.

I then wrote a half dozen more stories including "The Birds & Bees in Beijing," "The Bridge," "Chimeras," "Chicken Blood Therapy," "The Jaundice Ward" and "Trojan Rooster," all of which I submitted for publication in various literary journals.

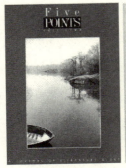  

For three years I heard nothing back until the spring of 1999 when "The Jaundice Ward" was accepted by Five Points, a literary journal published by Georgia State University. [3] I was reminded that Ha Jin had once published one of his stories in the same journal. In the letter of acceptance, the editor of **Five Points** compared my "The Jaundice Ward" to Ha Jin's story and expressed appreciation of my use of black humor. The story brought me a fortune of $135!

"The Birds & Bees in Beijing" was also accepted and published in the Spring 1999 issue of

---

[3] "The Jaundice Ward," the Fall 1999 (Vol.4 No.1) issue of Five Points

The Armchair Aesthete.[4] It was followed by "The Bridge" which appeared in the April 1999 issue of **Timber Creek Review**. [5]

"Chimeras" was published in the Summer 1999 issue of **Kimera: A Journal of Fine Writing**.[6] It was also accepted by **Michigan Quarterly Review and Baltimore Review**. I was pleasantly surprised to learn that "Chimeras" was nominated for the 1999 Pushcart Prize.

---

[4] "The Birds & Bees in Beijing," the Spring 1999 (No. 10) issue of The Armchair Aesthete

[5] "The Bridge," the April 1999 (Vol.5 No.4) issue of Timber Creek Review

[6] "Chimeras," the Summer 1999 (Vol.4 No.1) issue of Kimera: A Journal of Fine Writing

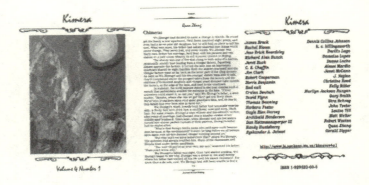

"Chicken Blood Therapy" was published in the Winter 1999 issue of **Pangolin Papers**,[7] and was also nominated for the 1999 Pushcart Prize. It was later published as a reprint in the Spring 2000 issue of **The Edge City Review**.

The last story I wrote in 1995 was "Trojan Rooster," a story created in laughter. It was

---

[7] "Chicken Blood Therapy," the Winter 1999 (Vol.6 No.2) issue of Pangolin Papers

published in the Fall 2002 issue of **The Minnesota Review**.[8]

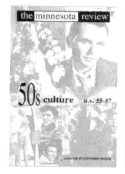

In 1996, I wrote a novel titled <u>Three-Legged Red-Crowned Crane</u> which has now been edited and renamed <u>Expatriates</u>. Some chapters of Expatriates were published as short stories along with the publication of my other English language short stories written in 1995. The second chapter, for example, was published as "Flight" in the June 28, 1999 issue of the Canadian journal **Christian Courier**.[9]

---

[8] "Trojan Rooster," the Fall 2002 (Nos. 55-56) issue of The Minnesota Review

[9] "Flight," June 18, 1999 (No.2615), Christian Courier, also accepted by The Banner.

The third chapter was published as "Defection" in the September 1999 issue of **Words of Wisdom**. [10]

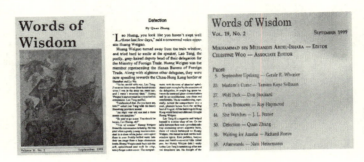

The fourteenth chapter was published as "Inspection" in the 2001 winter issue of **Red Rock Review**. [11]

---

[10] "Defection," September 1999 (Vol.19 No.2), Words of Wisdom

[11] "Inspection," Winter 2001(Vol.1 No.9) Red Rock Review

The fifteenth chapter was published as "Boomerang" in the March 2000 issue of **The Long Story**. [12]

---

[12] " Boomerang," March 2000 (No.18,) The Long Story

TROJAN ROOSTER

No one knows how it all happened. The casual crow of a single rooster one day led to the cacophony of a multitude the next, and transformed the entire, impenetrable and dignified Guofu Dayuan, the State Council's residential compound in Beijing, known as the Quad, into a chicken farm. Designed in the early 1950s by our ex-friends, Russian bunker engineers, with perhaps an imminent World War III in mind, the Quad was built to be capable of withstanding a limited military assault from outside. This was very much in evidence not only in the massive, seamless quadrilateral design itself but also in the unique construction of the one, tunnel-like gateway, the only gateway into the entire Quad with its more than four hundred families.

Ever since that first rooster was smuggled into the citadel, the idea of using chicken blood as a therapy broke out and spread like a disease.

Word passed quickly from the toothless to the toothy that by injecting chicken blood intravenously into the body, all health problems, known and unknown, would vanish. It was THE wonder drug that people, over the centuries, had been searching for. Chicken blood built up the vital energies and nourished the blood. It rejuvenated the old and invigorated the young, strengthened the immune system and restored the life juices. Some even said that it was mentioned in the Bencaoganmu, that is, The Compendium of Materia Medica, the most ancient and authoritative book on Chinese herbal medicine, even though no one had ever read it. No wonder the residents of the Quad embraced the idea with such unprecedented vigor and spontaneity. Their performance in all the political movements in the decade since the Liberation in 1949 paled to mediocrity by comparison.

Overnight, chickens of all sizes were brought into this most discriminatory habitat. Whether on the cold cement floors in cramped rooms in the most visible, bunker-like buildings which had been built at minimal cost without ostensibly violating the architectural harmony of the Quad, or on the well-waxed and carpeted wood floors in spacious five room apartments in the secluded, red-brick buildings with carved and painted green eaves and sloping, golden-tiled roofs, roosters proved themselves masters of highest adaptability. They bickered in large, impressive cement balconies and strutted leisurely down narrower stairways and darker hallways. They chased each other in and out of kitchens and bathrooms, shared or private. They got along with captains, majors, colonels and generals just as fine as with their secretaries, cooks, gardeners and chauffeurs.

When the Quad's most respected residents, the solemn bureau chiefs and section directors, silver-haired or bald-headed Army veterans and war heroes, such as Chief Tian, Commissar Gu, Major Zhou, Colonel Ma, General Zhang and Grandpa Meng, each began to carry a robust rooster under his arm, thereby joining the rank and file of their laughing and joking secretaries and chauffeurs who clutched their own roosters, it was generally considered that something had to be right about this craze for chicken blood.

What seemed to pass unnoticed, however, in this harmonious communal event was the active participation of the younger generation in the Quad. While the older people were preoccupied with drawing chicken blood to pump into their veins, the younger ones were engaged in a more bloody game of an entirely different nature. Each day, after their parents had done with the roosters and gone to work, the depleted roosters were, once again, taken out of their habitat and led to battle arenas scattered throughout the Quad. There, they would meet opponents chosen for them and would fight for their lives. With over four hundred families in the Quad, there was no lack of children and teens willing to risk the lives of their parents' miracle chickens to fulfill their own insatiable cravings for participation in heroic and bloody battle.

As during the period of the Warring States in our ancient history, wars were declared without any justifiable cause and fought with intense ruthlessness. After the thunder and lightning of each fight, when the dust had settled and the injured roosters had retreated, the battlegrounds inside the Quad were littered with chicken feathers and blood. Some roosters would never return to the abode of their masters, humble or luxurious.

Among the first to fall in battle were roosters bearing carelessly assigned names such as Butcher or Bandit. Then came the second batch with foreign names such as Napoleon, Hitler or Genghis Khan. And, for the sake of record keeping, it was noted that General Zhang's Genghis Khan was slaughtered by Yankee, the rooster belonging to the General's bodyguard, Uncle Du. It was said that the death of Genghis Khan caused General Zhang consternation as well as constipation. As the highest-ranking resident in the Quad, the General had also been the most zealous advocate of the new fad. He was the one who'd sworn to the efficacy of chicken blood by the authority of the famous Compendium. But what upset the General most was the interruption of his secret plan to save the Zhang family name from extinction. The General had become convinced that the blood of the right-sized rooster could cure his daughter-in-law's infertility. Genghis Khan had, therefore, been carefully chosen for that purpose and had been brought back from the General's home village hundreds of miles away in Shandong province. With the death of Genghis Khan, it was said, the General never again felt quite safe around his bodyguard.

The demise of Major Zhou's Hitler had greater repercussions. Hitler was publicly humiliated and literally torn apart by Monkey King before his blood could be further drawn for better use. The humiliation was intensified by the fact that Monkey King belonged to Major Zhou's own chauffeur, Uncle Liu and Liu's son, Dabin.

The loss of Hitler was a big blow to Major Zhou. Rumor had it that Hitler might've been that very first rooster that got smuggled into the Quad against city ordinances, though the Major never publicly admitted it. But the Major was among the first to credit the cure of his kidney problem and his high-blood pressure to the rooster's blood. For the loss of Hitler, thirteen-year old Zhou Wei was soundly whipped, in front of a crowd of his peers, by his bald father, the Major, in the beautiful little backyard garden attached to his brick home. Zhou Wei's screams seemed to echo for days in the Quad.

"Liu Dabin, you Bunker Dweller," shouted Zhou Wei between his screams. I will break your Monkey King's neck one of these days!" Zhou Wei had always been a poor loser.

The incident was probably the biggest embarrassment in Zhou Wei's life. He who could barely get along with other kids whose parents had chauffeured cars, had now lost a chicken fight to a mere bunker-dweller, the son of his father's chauffeur. What was more, he'd gotten a public whipping. Zhou Wei knew that he himself was nicknamed "Hitler" by the children in the Quad. By naming his own rooster Hitler, and pitting him against Liu Dabin's Monkey King, Zhou Wei had made a serious gamble. To his great disappointment, Hitler proved to be one of those noncombative chickens, vicious in appearance but weak inside.

Monkey King was, on the other hand, a lot truer to the idiosyncrasies of his namesake, harmless and playful in appearance but ferocious and sneaky once in for a fight. Liu Dabin had never been so proud and elated. For years he'd been called "Bunker Dweller" and other worse names by Zhou Wei. Now his Monkey King, he thought, had finally taught the brat a lesson.

The death of Hitler brought the Warring States Period to an end, but it immediately ushered in the Period of Division, though divisions were never drawn without great irony. Roosters, now acquired in multiple numbers, were pitted against each other in teams. For a week, the roosters that Chief Tian, Head of the Bureau of Administrative Affairs, had brought from his home village in Anhui province were clear winners in the Quad. Chief Tian's three sons were, for the first time, willing publicly to acknowledge their ancestral roots though Anhui was mainly renowned in the country for its poverty. The Tian Brothers called the troop of their three roosters the "Nian Army," a famous Anhui peasant army that rose against the last dynasty in the middle of the 19th century. To their credit, the Nian roosters did dethrone an Emperor, a rooster which belonged to sixty-five-year-old Grandpa Meng, who himself was one of Chairman Mao's stretcher-bearers during the

Long March in the early 1930s.

But the dominance of the Nian Army was soon challenged and quickly undermined by a group of roosters freshly brought in from Shandong province by Chief Tian's army buddy and colleague, Commissar Gu. Following in the footsteps of General Zhang, the owner of Genghis Khan, Commissar Gu made a hasty trip back to his home village. A week later, to the delight of his four daughters, Papa Gu brought back four feisty mountain roosters. In keeping with the trend set by Chief Tian's sons, Commissar Gu's daughters named their roosters "Boxers" after the army of peasants and handicraftsmen from Shandong and its neighboring provinces that had fought the foreign imperialist forces in 1900.

The near massacre of the Nian Army by the Boxers was an enormous embarrassment to the two good old friends, Chief Tian and Commissar Gu. They suggested a compromise. As a result, a new alliance was formed. From that day on, Chief Tian's three sons and Commissar Gu's four daughters strutted around the Quad with their newly combined army of seven fully recuperated and feisty roosters. Since their fathers were veterans of the Anti-Japanese War, the children of the two families were able to agree right away to name their allied forces the "Eighth Route Army," a famous peasant army led by the Chinese Communist Party in the eight-year War of Resistance Against Japan from 1937 to 1945.

Knowing the ferocious nature of Liu Dabin's Monkey King and knowing also that an encounter with Hitler's killer was imminent, the children made a smart move and lobbied Liu Dabin to enlist Monkey King as commander-in-chief of their allied forces. With Dabin's approval, the formation of the Eighth Route Army was complete and the numbers perfect -- eight roosters to eight boys and girls.

For quite a while, the Eighth Route Army appeared to be invincible. They beat another allied force newly organized by Colonel Ma's daughter with the three sons of the Colonel's chauffeur, Uncle Zheng. The defeat stunned the Ma and Zheng children who were only glad that they hadn't publicized the name of their troop yet. The annals of revolutionary war would not be marred by the record of an internecine battle between the Eighth Route Army and the New Fourth Army, another famous army also led by the Chinese Communist Party.

The Eighth Route Army continued their sweep to total victory throughout the Quad. They defeated Uncle Han's Outlaws and outsmarted the Eight Immortals belonging to young and pretty Aunty Dai. According to classical myth, the Eight Immortals each had a special, magic talent. It turned out, however, that each of Auntie Dai's Eight Immortals was too egotistical to help the other during the fight. When they met the onslaught from the collective effort of the Eighth Route Army, their individual talents didn't quite pan out as hoped.

Like a sharp knife cutting through tofu, the Eighth Route Army smashed all possible resistance and achieved complete dominance. The Period of Division ended in peace and tranquility and, for the first time in weeks, the Quad ceased to ring with murderous shouts.

Then, one early morning, the residents were

awakened by a strange, muffled bass-like crow. It sounded so low and menacing that it sent cold shivers down everyone's spine. The sound came from Major Zhou's beautiful little backyard garden. Within minutes, the rumor that Zhou Wei had issued an ultimatum to Liu Dabin spread like a prairie fire. Even before the sun had quite risen, the murmured rumor had been confirmed.

That day, at four o'clock in the afternoon, an hour after school and two hours before their parents got off work, a large, noisy crowd of kids had already gathered like mosquitoes in the Quad's center court where there was a well-tended, long, oblong flower bed as well as a big, circular flower bed with a cement border and a fountain in the middle.

In the center of the crowd, on the pavement between the two flower beds, stood a shiny black rooster with a blood-red comb, a spectacular black tail and sharp, fearless eyes. It was the size of a twenty-five-pound turkey.

"Liu Dabin," shouted Zhou Wei, "bring out your Monkey King! Let him meet Silent Thunder!

The best from Japan!" Sweat soaked the hair on Zhou Wei's forehead and darkened the collar of his short-sleeved, blue athletic shirt. "Give in now or you'll pay for it, you stupid Bunker Dweller!"

A few yards away stood Liu Dabin, flanked by three agitated Tian brothers and four angry Gu sisters. Behind him was Monkey King and the rest of the Eighth Route Army which now looked pitifully dwarfed in comparison with Silent Thunder. The latter glanced about, bored and nonchalant.

"Dabin, don't be afraid," shouted one of the stalwart Zheng brothers. "Fight the foreign devil!"

"That's right!" muttered the Gu sisters, as the Tian brothers nudged Dabin forward. "Destroy the enemy!"

"Down with the Japanese imperialist invader!" shouted another Zheng brother.

The shout was taken up right away by the encroaching crowd of excited children. Finally, Liu Dabin stepped aside to let Monkey King enter the circle.

Monkey King, short, brown and sturdy, strutted forward and came to a full stop. He stared silently at Silent Thunder. Then, instead of doing a forward leap and somersault which had been one of his ritualistic, pre-battle bluffs to confuse and surprise his opponent, he ran a big circle around the giant sumo, did a flying, backward flip, and vanished suddenly into the growing crowd of young spectators. Seeing this, Monkey King's lieutenants rose with one mighty squawk and exited after their leader.

For a brief moment, the crowd stood in shocked silence.

"You lost, you lost! Your Monkey King's a coward. So's your Eighth Route Army!" crowed Zhou Wei.

The defeat of the Eighth Route Army by Silent Thunder, a Japanese rooster, was felt like a national humiliation among the kids in the Quad. For days, Commissar Gu's four daughters were in tears while Chief Tian's three sons and Liu Dabin sulked in their respective rooms. The other children walked around looking serious and sullen. To their dismay, living in the same enclosed Quad, they were awakened every morning by the distinctive, monstrous crow of

Silent Thunder, a constant reminder of humiliation and defeat.

Then, one day Silent Thunder fell silent. A rumor spread that he'd succumbed to the chicken pestilence. However, the jubilation among the kids in the Quad didn't last very long, as rooster after rooster followed suit. Within a week, the pestilence had wiped out the entire rooster population. Among the last to go was the disgraced champion, Monkey King, along with his loyal, feisty roosters known as the Eighth Route Army.

It took a little while for the Quad residents to recover from their collective loss. Though the fad for chicken blood perished, its effect on the residents' lives seemed to give some credence to its reported powers. For the sake of record keeping, it was noted that right after the death of Silent Thunder, Major Zhou was once again hospitalized for his recurring kidney problem though his blood pressure remained satisfactory. General Zhang's daughter-in-law had a miscarriage, but the General was optimistic because he was now convinced that drinking black tea three times a day would enhance fertility.

The Quad residents noticed that Colonel Ma had exchanged his favorite faded, olive green army uniform for a light grey civilian suit, but no one was sure whether or not this was directly related to the roosters. Chief Tian was said to have laid down a law strictly forbidding any reference to roosters either at home or at the office. Commissar Gu appeared to spend more and more time in his own office and away from his wife and four daughters. Sixty-five-year-old, silver-haired Grandpa Meng had recovered his youthful vigor. He'd been seen one day, lying naked in bed, with thirty-five-year-old Aunty Dai. Rumor had it that they'd been like that since the chicken blood fad had started.

The younger generation in the Quad seemed less affected, not having had chicken blood pumped into their veins. With the end of the chicken wars, they returned to life as usual, except that Liu Dabin was now called Monkey King and Zhou Wei's nickname had become Collaborator.

Chicken Blood Therapy

The moment Commissar Gu Zhengfa stepped into his apartment, he regretted his decision to return early from his quiet, tree-shaded office at the Bureau of Administrative Affairs under the State Council in Beijing. The front door of the apartment opened into a dark, narrow hall that led directly to the kitchen.

"Chickens are chickens, Mom. They're not a miracle drug," said a brash young voice in the kitchen. His second daughter, thirteen-year-old Gu Na, was squabbling with his wife, Chen Ping, again. Every time they fought, it was over something he didn't care about one way or the other.

"Lao Gu!" said Chen Ping. His wife's high-pitched voice stopped Gu Zhengfa before he could make a getaway to his study.

"Have you heard how Major Zhou has cured his kidney problem? His wife told me it was the chicken blood that saved his life. Remember two weeks ago he said he was going to have an operation? They've cancelled the appointment. You know why? His kidney problem has disappeared and even his high-blood pressure is gone. Don't you think it's amazing, eh?"

Lao Gu knew how he was supposed to answer. Shuffling into the kitchen, he said, "Yes, yes. It does sound pretty amazing, Lao Chen. We do seem to live in an age of miracles, don't we? Who would've believed, a year ago, that eggshells could cure arthritis when you first said so? Now people with the problem eat nothing but eggshells. As far as chicken blood is concerned, put it in soup, and it'll taste just as good as bean curd." Lao Gu wished, with all his heart, that he'd stayed at the office. There, at least, as head of the bureau's Party Committee, he was the boss.

"Mom's not talking about chicken blood in soup, Dad," said Gu Na, sharply. "Though it sounds just as gross. She's talking about having fresh chicken blood injected into you intravenously. When that happens, all your health problems disappear. It's a cure-all. Doesn't that sound familiar to you, Dad?"

"I don't know what's gotten into her, Lao Gu." Chen Ping was visibly upset. "Gu Na is such a scoffer. She only believes in herself." She turned to Gu Na, and said, "If you're so smart, Second Daughter, tell me when I've been wrong. Remember, I was the first to say that raw eggs were good for the health? Now you see how many people can't live without them?"

"Yes, Mom. Major Zhou for one. But, don't forget we all got sick one time and almost died."

When Gu Zhengfa's three other daughters, Gu Hua, the eldest and the twins, Gu Jia and Gu Wa, joined the rest of the family around the dinner table that night, the subject of chickens was brought up again. Lao Gu had barely sat down, when his wife started complaining.

"I think your head needs a good scrubbing out, Lao Gu. You're getting too stubborn to accept any new ideas." Chen Ping slammed a large dish of fried tomatoes and eggs on the table beside another dish of diced cucumber blended with salt and plenty of crushed garlic.

Before Lao Gu got a chance to reply, Gu

Jia, one of the twins, said, "I heard you guys were talking about chicken blood a while ago in the kitchen. It's the 60s! Let's not have any more superstitions."

Gu Wa, the other twin, objected. "I don't see why we can't talk about chicken blood. The topic is an excellent appetizer. Mom wants chicken blood and Dad doesn't object. Great. Looks like we're going to be the healthiest family in the compound." Both twins, in short pigtails, plunged chopsticks into the cucumbers.

"You should be ashamed of yourselves," said Gu Hua, the eldest daughter. It was her responsibility to control her siblings. 'Why can't you just eat quietly like Dad."

Lao Gu sighed as he reached for the cucumbers. He avoided looking at anyone.

In his office the next day, Gu Zhengfa was surprised when Lao Tian, Chief of the Bureau of Administrative Affairs, asked him whether he liked the idea of chicken blood therapy.

"Lao Gu," said Lao Tian, "I know you're like me. I'm usually the last person to believe in these medical fads. But this time, Lao Gu, I think it's not as totally off-track as it sounds. Last night, General Zhang phoned me. When I mentioned the recent craze for chicken blood in our compound -- you know what? -- he said he'd just come back from a trip to his home village in Shandong. He went back for the sole purpose of looking for the right-sized roosters! He's convinced that rooster blood can cure his daughter-in-law's infertility. He says it's in the Bencaoganmu. And you and I both know that's been the best book on Chinese herbal medicine for thousands of years, Lao Gu."

Lao Gu could almost hear his own heart pounding. For seventeen years, ever since he'd married Chen Ping, he'd harbored a passionate and secret yearning for a son of his own. Not even the news of Chen Ping's medical complications had lessened the intensity of his desire. But Chen Ping was approaching forty, and Lao Gu was beginning to see hope slip away. Lao Tian's news about General Zhang rekindled a dying spark. Lao Gu decided that all the years of thinking about a son had to end.

That night, after dinner and before the girls

began to clean up, Lao Gu made an announcement in a voice he hadn't used in a long time, the voice of an army deputy regiment commander. "I want everyone here to listen carefully to what I have to say. Your Mom is right about the chicken blood therapy. It's been recorded in the Bencaoganmu and practiced by our ancestors for thousands of years. In view of your Mom's poor health and medical complications, I've decided to take a trip back to my home village to bring back some real roosters to cure her."

Chen Ping was dumbfounded. Not since they were married, had Lao Gu ever made a decision without consulting her first. Nor had he ever breached their marriage agreement never to return to his home village without her permission. And Chen Ping had never given him her permission. Chen Ping began to regret her enthusiasm for chicken blood.

Before Chen Ping could recover from her astonishment, Gu Na said, "Think about it. We've been practicing chicken blood therapy for thousands of years. Our ancestors must've invented the intravenous injection."

"Enough of your smartness, girl," said Gu Hua. "This is serious. Mom, do you really think the chicken blood would help?"

Gu Jia began to whine. "Daddy, please take me with you. I won't cause you any trouble. I know exactly what's good for Mom. The bigger the chicken the better."

"I don't see why Dad can't take us all for a ride," Gu Wa suggested simultaneously.

Lao Gu was unmoved. Silently, he reached for a piece of salt-and-garlic cucumber.

After dinner, Gu Zhengfa stole into his study. There, behind the closed door and in a comforting cloud of smoke from his Zhonghua brand cigarette, the best kind in China, he thought, with a tiny thrill, of Chen Ping's surprise and agitation at his announcement. For seventeen years she'd successfully prevented him from returning to his home village. When they'd first met, in 1949, Chen Ping was a twenty-two-year-old university graduate. She was pretty, and had the liveliness of a well-educated, outgoing city girl. As a thirty three-year-old deputy regiment commander in the army, Lao

Gu was then in his prime, full of vigor and ambition. They hit it off together right away. Finally, one day, Lao Gu had to confess to Chen Ping that he was a married man. He'd been married a year before he left his village in 1941 to join the Anti-Japanese Army. That was the last time he'd seen his wife, Yumei.

The news hadn't seemed to bother Chen Ping. Many of her college friends had married army officers like Lao Gu, men with existing marital ties in their home villages. It'd all been done in the name of a popular movement called Fanbaoban, a movement launched to oppose traditional, arranged marriages. Thus, Gu Zhengfa and Chen Ping's application for permission to marry had been approved by their superiors without the slightest hitch.

Lao Gu inhaled the smoke from his cigarette deeply into his lungs. He'd never thought about lung cancer. Recently, he'd noticed that his grey hair had started to turn white, yet he was barely past fifty. Chen Ping blamed it on his smoking. "Those cigarettes of yours have drained all the darkness from your hair into your lungs," she said. Lao Gu wasn't convinced. His army buddy, silver-haired Lao Tian had never smoked in his life. Gu Zhengfa tried, but failed, to figure out what had happened to his marriage, to the lively young girl Chen Ping used to be. If General Zhang's Shandong roosters could cure the daughter-in-law's infertility, thought Lao Gu, maybe Shandong roosters would give him the son he and Chen Ping wanted.

A week later, on his return from his visit to his home village, as Lao Gu was driven by the State Council's chauffeur through the gates of the residential compound, he noticed that the compound had changed. Chickens of all sizes were everywhere. They strutted leisurely through the halls, bickered in the balconies, and chased each other in and out of the buildings. The entire compound looked, sounded and smelled like a chicken farm.

Gu Jia, one of the twins, was the first to greet him at the door of the apartment. She caught sight of the roosters Lao Gu had brought back from the home village, and the girl's eyes grew round with wonder and desire. "Mom, Dad's back," Gu

Jia finally managed to shout. 'Wow, look at those roosters. I bet no one has ever seen any like them before. Can I have one, Dad? Please?" Her three sisters jammed the entrance, each wanting to take a peek at the newcomers. Lao Gu frowned, and then pulled together a weak smile. He handed them two rooster coops and headed for the shower.

Another week passed, and Chen Ping noticed, with some alarm, that Lao Gu hadn't yet shaken off the depression that had beset him since his return. He left his study only to eat and to go to work. He told his family that he was "writing a report," which meant that he was not to be disturbed. The change in Lao Gu didn't escape the eyes of his two older daughters.

"What's happened to Dad?" Gu Hua asked her mother a few days later. "Didn't he get what he wanted? Why does he look so glum all the time?"

"Your Dad's just tired. A week's travel has taken all the energy out of him. He'll be all right after a while." From the faces of Gu Hua and Gu Na, Chen Ping knew she hadn't convinced them.

"Dad's sure strange," said Gu Na. "I never

thought he'd take something like chicken blood therapy so seriously. All of a sudden, he bends over backwards to get chickens. And a week later, after he's gone to all that trouble to bring back those humongous roosters, he's lost interest."

Gu Na's remark added to Chen Ping's frustration. Old Gu refused to discuss his trip with her. But, every Wednesday afternoon, he insisted on accompanying her to the clinic in the compound.

Gu Zhengfa began to spend more and more time at his office. One day after work, Lao Tian popped in to talk to him.

"Lao Gu, I heard from my son that you brought back some gorgeous roosters for your daughters. My son says if I don't get him some like yours soon, he's going to move in with you. Ha! Ha! Ha!" Lao Tian, silver-haired and stout, in short sleeves and shapeless, army green trousers, was obviously proud of everything about his youngest son.

"You've got some real fighters, Lao Gu," continued the bureau chief. "You should hear what my son says. Those roosters of yours are now the compound's champions. Ours isn't a small compound either. No one has beaten your roosters yet. They fight like crazy."

"Are you joking, Lao Tian? You mean my daughters are using Chen Ping's roosters to fight?" asked Lao Gu in surprise. "I never know what's going on anymore. To tell you the truth, though, I don't particularly care what they do with those chickens. Everyone seems to be after their blood anyway. I don't understand this obsession with chickens. Isn't there anything else for us to think about in our lives?"

Lao Tian detected a note of bitterness in Gu Zhengfa's voice.

"Are you all right, Lao Gu? Is something bothering you? Can I help you?"

"No, no. It's nothing. I think I'm just a little tired. I'll be fine in a few days," said Lao Gu.

Lao Tian left, and Gu Zhengfa continued to sit at his desk in his smoke-filled office. The room was dark, except for the red glow of the tip of his cigarette. Lao Gu had lost all sense of how often his mind had gone back to prowl among the images of his trip home.

"*Ah, Zhengfa. Is that really you? So you're not dead. You've come back home. I can't see clearly anymore. Too old. But I know your voice.*" *The hoarse sound of an old man replied to Lao Gu's inquiry.*

Lao Gu peered through thick, choking smoke from the straw-burning stove. In the dark room, lit only by a small kerosene lamp, he caught the outline of his uncle's almost naked, hunched back as the seventy-five-year-old man propped himself up from the kang on which he'd been lying. As Lao Gu moved closer to take the old man's thin, extended hand, he was surprised to see that his uncle still wore his hair in a long queue coiled on his head, in the style of the last dynasty. In the quarter of a century since Lao Gu had left the village, that queue had turned from black to white. An acrid smell of chickens, burning straw and unwashed human bodies filled the small, mud-floored room.

"*Zhengfa, you must be tired and hungry after that long trip from the Capital,*" *said his uncle.* "*If you don't mind your poor uncle's home, you can sleep with us after your aunt fixes something for you to eat." Lao Gu noticed that his uncle still used the old Qing dynasty term for Beijing. His uncle pointed a long-handled pipe towards a short, skinny grey-haired woman sitting inconspicuously, in the shadows, at the other end of the kang.*

"Aunty," said Lao Gu, bowing in a greeting.

"Zhengfa," said his aunt, "I certainly wouldn't have been able to recognize you.

How many years have you been away? You must have left a long, long time ago. Even before your parents died in the Japanese bombing. That was at least twenty-five years ago, wasn't it?" His aunt was still sharp-minded.

Gu Zhengfa had heard about the death of his parents from a fellow villager shortly after the bombing. The villager had joined Lao Gu's regiment, and had told him that practically the whole village had been wiped out.

"Yes, Aunty. It's been a long time. Over twenty-five years. I didn't know both you and uncle were still alive until now. I guess you were among the few lucky ones."

"Yes, I suppose so. Though I'm not sure how lucky we were, to tell you the truth, Zhengfa." Lao Gu's uncle spoke almost unintelligibly, in the village accent, from the gap between his toothless gums and his pipe. 'We've only barely survived. These last few years have been very hard." His uncle's thin, humped-back body shook with a racking cough. "Those of us who survived the wars ... so many died in the natural disasters a couple of years ago. Your wife, Zhengfa. She died then. There was nothing to eat. She died from the Goddess of Mercy clay she ate."

Gu Zhengfa felt as if somewhere inside him something had ripped wide open.

He'd heard that Yumei had survived the bombings and the civil war, but that was all he knew. Somehow, he'd persuaded himself that she'd remarried and was doing well in the new China.

"We all thought you'd died in the war," said Lao Gu's aunt. "Except for Yumei. Even when she was dying, she was sure you'd come back to see your son, Shuanzi. You've never seen him, have you? He was born eight months after you left the village.

He'll be so happy to see his father!"

In his office, Gu Zhengfa lit yet another cigarette. Through the smoke and by the bright moonlight from the window, he saw that it was 11:30 by his little desk clock. He decided to stay in his office for the night.

COLONEL MA'S FATHER

Ma Hongfu had left the army a long time ago, but his friends and colleagues still called him Colonel. For more than a decade, now, since the early 50s, he'd been serving as the chief of the Bureau of Internal Affairs under the State Council in Beijing. Colonel Ma liked to wear his army uniform, without its insignia and hat. The color, the shape, the feel and even the smell of the cloth made him feel complacent. After all he'd spent more of his life in the army than in the office.

Colonel Ma was a simple and orderly man. Every morning, he would get up at six o'clock. Fifteen minutes later, he would start his morning walk inside the State Council's residential compound. He always wore the same clean, military dress for all occasions, a four-pocketed jacket designating an officer, a pair of baggy trousers, both a faded, olive green, and a pair of black cloth shoes with white soles. Although he was more than fifty years old now, he walked with a straight back and powerful strides. At seven o'clock, he would be back in his five-room apartment on the second floor and ready for breakfast prepared by his wife, Yao Luyun. One steamed bun and one big bowl of thick corn porridge with some pickled vegetables was all he ate, no more and no less. At seven thirty, carrying his black leather portfolio, he would walk to the old but gleaming, black pre-Liberation Chevrolet parked outside his apartment, greet his chauffeur Lao Zheng and head for the bureau. The Colonel ate his lunch and took his nap at the bureau. After eight hours at the office, around five, he would return in his car to the compound. At six, Luyun would lay out the three-dishes-and-one-soup dinner for them both. And after that, the Colonel would spend a half hour watching TV or listening to the radio and two hours in his study, reading and writing. Lights in Colonel Ma's apartment would go out at ten sharp.

In more than a decade, ever since he'd started to work as the bureau chief, Colonel Ma had never changed his routine. Not even when his only daughter, Lanlan, was born. She was six years old now, and still in the State Council kindergarten in the western suburb of Beijing. She spent only the weekends with the Colonel and his wife.

Colonel Ma had been trying to get his father to come to live with him ever since his mother had passed away ten years ago, but to no avail. He wanted badly to give his father a comfortable home in Beijing. It was his only unfulfilled desire. One Spring, the Colonel's father finally agreed to come, and Colonel Ma went to his home village in Henan province to escort his short, bent, seventy-four-year-old father to Beijing. After a few days of necessary readjustment, the Colonel resumed his routine fully satisfied with all things.

Two weeks after his father's arrival, however, Colonel Ma received a call at his office from Luyun. During the ten o'clock break she'd left the hospital where she worked as a doctor and returned to their apartment to fetch some papers she'd forgotten. She told Colonel Ma that she couldn't find his father anywhere. She'd even searched the compound. Colonel Ma reassured his wife by saying that after two weeks of rest, his father might have gotten a little bored and gone out to explore the place by himself.

Colonel Ma was right. When he returned home early from the bureau that afternoon, he found his father dozing comfortably in bed in his own room. At the dinner table, the Colonel found an opportunity to talk to his father.

"Dad, are you feeling all right? Is there anything Luyun and I can do for you? If you don't like the lunch Luyun brings back from our compound dining hall, we can always hire someone to cook for you and for us if you like."

"I'm all right, son. Don't worry about me. I know how to take care of myself," said the Colonel's father, peremptorily.

"Beijing is a big city, Dad," said Luyun. "We've been here more than ten years now, and we still don't know the city that well ourselves. If you feel like seeing anything, Hongfu can ask Lao Zheng to take us around on Sundays."

Colonel Ma's brows twitched. He'd made it a rule that the car was to be used only for office related matters. For over ten years, there'd never been an exception. Even Luyun went to work by bus every day.

"Don't bother anyone for my sake," said the Colonel's father. "I don't care too much for Beijing, except for the Forbidden City. That's the only thing I want to see. After I see that, you can go wherever you want. I'll stay at home." With that, he abruptly terminated the conversation.

The following Sunday, Colonel Ma took his father, along with Luyun and Lanlan, to the Forbidden City. The tour went pleasantly for everyone and when they got home, Lanlan almost missed the special bus back to her kindergarten. After returning to the quiet, spacious apartment, the Colonel's father announced that his life-long wish had been fulfilled. He wasn't interested in anything else and would prefer to be left alone thereafter. Colonel Ma and Luyun looked at each other.

"Forgive our thoughtlessness, Dad," said Luyun. "Maybe we shouldn't have arranged this outing before you were fully recovered from your long trip to Beijing. Next time, you let us know when you're ready to go out, OK Dad?"

"I'm satisfied with this visit. I only wanted to see where the Emperor lived, that's all. Now I've done that, I don't mind whether I go back home or stay here a little longer if you both don't mind." Colonel Ma's father leaned back complacently in an armchair.

"Of course, we don't mind, Dad," said Luyun. "You can stay as long as you want, right Hongfu?"

"Luyun's right, Dad," said Colonel Ma. "This is your home. You do whatever you like. If you feel lonely during the day, we can bring Lanlan back from the kindergarten to keep you company." The Colonel turned to his wife and asked, "Don't you think that would be a good idea, Luyun?"

"That would certainly make Lanlan happy. Look how well she gets along with you, Dad. I haven't seen her so sorry to go back to kindergarten in a long time. Anyway, she's almost seven. She'll be ready for elementary school this Fall," said Luyun.

From his father's silence, Colonel Ma inferred that the idea of bringing Lanlan back suited him perfectly.

Lanlan was delighted to be back with Grandpa. Luyun noticed that every night after dinner, Lanlan would spend hours with Grandpa on the balcony, talking, laughing, and pestering him to tell her stories. Lanlan looked healthier, too, even after only one week. One night, after she'd cleaned away the dinner dishes, Luyun went to Colonel Ma in his study and told him her little observation.

"It looks like Lanlan and Dad get along very well," she said. "It's good for both of them. Lanlan doesn't look as frail as before, and Dad has been in a much better mood ever since."

"Dad's been alone for too long. He wasn't like that before Mom passed away. I'm glad Lanlan can keep him company," said the Colonel with a sense of relief.

Colonel Ma had noticed his father's changing mood, too. He noticed other things as well, things like his ashtray being cleaned out every day. It used to be his job to dump the ashes out when it was full. One day, he also found that his shovel and hammer were missing from the utility closet. He kept all these minute findings to himself and went about his routine as usual.

Two more weeks passed. Colonel Ma was pleased to hear from Luyun that Lanlan had started to learn from Grandpa how to wash her own clothes and sew on buttons. He couldn't help being a little jealous of his daughter, for he noticed that his father had a lot more to say to her than to him. Lanlan, too, was growing distant as she clung to her Grandpa. Like the other day, he noticed, when he asked her what she did with Grandpa during the day, Lanlan had hesitated for a second and then run away from him with a mischievous laugh. Not that he'd meant to be nosy. His inquiry had been entirely innocent. For a second, he'd felt uncomfortable. But he did notice that Lanlan had become less of a spoiled city baby.

A month later, in the hallway of the building for Administrative Affairs, the Colonel bumped into the deputy Party boss of the bureau, Lao Tang.

"Colonel Ma, I've been looking for you all morning," said Lao Tang. He quickly scanned the hallway to make sure that no one was within earshot and resumed his conversation in a subdued voice.

"Excuse me for what I have to tell you, Colonel. As I was leaving our compound in the car this morning, I saw someone who looked a lot like your father at the dump site. There was a little girl of Lanlan's age with him. I might be wrong, Colonel, but I thought you might want to know about it."

Colonel Ma was dumfounded. He looked quickly at his Swiss watch, given to him by one of his old army buddies serving now as ambassador to Denmark. It was a quarter to ten. He rushed into his office, told his secretary to cancel the ten o'clock meeting, and called Lao Zheng, his chauffeur, to drive him home right away.

In the car, Colonel Ma tried to collect his thoughts. He'd responded, without thinking, to what he viewed as a potential crisis, though he wasn't quite sure of its nature. Why was he panicking? Wasn't he just afraid that Lao Tang might be right, and that his father and his daughter were really going through the residential compound's dump site collecting trash? And if they were, what should he do about it? Tell them to stop, because he was the Colonel, a bureau chief, a well-respected, high-ranking Communist cadre, and he couldn't stand the embarrassment? Wouldn't that offend his father's pride and hurt his daughter? Why were they doing it? Hadn't he offered to give his father anything he wanted? And what if Luyun were to find out about the trash collecting, and find out, too, that he'd done nothing to stop it? What would people think?

The cigarette in his hand burnt his fingers before dying out. Colonel Ma quickly dusted off the ashes from his sleeves and trousers. He gently tapped his chauffeur on the right shoulder and said, "Lao Zheng, never mind. Let's go back to the bureau, now."

Colonel Ma's black Chevrolet returned to the compound at five that afternoon. He didn't go home right away. After bidding goodbye to Lao Zheng, he went for a walk. He needed some quietness to think clearly. Following a footpath and going through a side-door, the Colonel found himself wandering around the stretch of unused land between the back of the compound and the old moat that encircled the city walls. He was surprised to see a part of the land, less than 500 square feet, fenced in by bamboo poles and metal wires. Inside the fence, the wild grass was gone. The hitherto barren earth was now well harrowed, watered, and planted with corn, sunflowers, castor-oil plants, and a variety of vegetables such as string-beans, tomatoes, cucumbers and squashes. In one corner of this yard, stood a small, wooden shed. The shed had no windows, and the door was shut. Colonel Ma hadn't been behind the compound for quite some time. He wondered, now, who could be the owner of the new yard. Walking up to the shed, he peered through a gap between the boards. He saw, against one of the walls, stacks of old newspapers and wastepaper of all kinds folded and piled up to the ceiling. Two large, worn-out wicker baskets were filled with old shoes and clothes. Some glass bottles of various sizes were shoved into a corner. And then, he saw his own shovel tilted against the wall beside a bamboo shoulder pole and two metal pails near the door.

The Colonel could almost see his bent old father and Lanlan squatting together in the shed and sorting out their baskets of trash from the dump before tilling and watering the vegetable garden together. But as he watched, the image shifted. Now he saw a seven-year old boy in tatters who clung tightly to his father's thin, calloused hand as they stood on a dusty road at the entrance of his small, home village in Henan province. That was more than forty years ago, when Henan and the neighboring provinces had been hit by famine because of wars among the warlords. His mother had stood at the door of their mud hut to watch them leave. He remembered that she was short and wore dark, homespun tatters. Clinging to her, and wailing, were his four, naked younger brothers and sisters. Father and son worked where they could in larger, neighboring villages or counties, sending money back home when possible. When work ran out, they joined others who were begging their way hundreds of miles north to the mines and forests of Manchuria. For years the father and son had worked, begged and slept in all sorts of places. Until one day he'd had enough. It was still dark, when he'd left his father sleeping on the ground at the dock in Qingdao city. He ran away. He soon found and joined the Red

Army. For the first time in his life he got enough to eat and something decent to wear.

That night after ten, Yao Luyun found her husband still in his study. At the dinner table, her husband had ducked her question when she'd casually asked what had kept him late for dinner. Now he was late for bed.

"Lao Ma, are you all right?" asked Luyun, as soon as she'd closed the study door behind her. "It's already past ten, and you're still here smoking. What's bothering you? Did something happen at the bureau?"

"Luyun, there's something I have to tell you." The Colonel sat up straight in his armchair. Through the smoke and in the dim light from a shaded lamp on the study desk, Yao Luyun noticed that her husband looked tired and perplexed.

"Dad is a very proud and honest man," said Colonel Ma. "And very independent, too." He was groping for the right words. "You know how much I've wanted him to come and stay with us. And Lanlan is getting along wonderfully with him. And now..." Colonel Ma's voice faded away. He had to tell her about the dump site and the garden. Luyun quickly touched the teacup on the little table beside her husband's armchair and went to the kitchen to heat up some water.

The following morning, Colonel Ma changed his routine. He got up at five thirty and spent an entire hour in the vegetable garden behind the compound. At a quarter to seven, he returned to his apartment a sweaty man. His army uniform was no longer neat and clean, and his shoes were covered with mud.

After taking a quick shower and breakfast, he walked to his car in a civilian suit, all in light grey with a pair of black leather shoes.

Lao Zheng was surprised. In more than ten years as the Colonel's chauffeur, he'd never seen the Colonel out of uniform.

"You sure look different, Colonel," said Lao Zheng, who still wasn't certain of his eyes. "Anywhere else, and I'd have thought I was picking up a stranger."

"You're right, Lao Zheng. I'm not the Colonel anymore. Like you, I'm just an ordinary man," answered Colonel Ma, meaning it as a joke. But in the car, he sat and thought. He thought of his father begging along the roadside. He thought, with shame, both of his desertion and, now, of his pride. The revolution had changed many things. He was happy to have his father with him again.

Colonel Ma and his wife maintained their silence even when the fresh vegetables and corn started to appear in a wicker basket on the tiled kitchen floor. Yao Luyun quietly washed them clean, made them into various tasty dishes and placed them on the table. The whole family sat facing each other around the dinner table and enjoyed the fresh garden supplies without betraying the least surprise. After dinner, the Colonel's father and Lanlan continued their storytelling on the balcony, and Colonel Ma and his wife resumed their usual tasks as if nothing out of the ordinary had happened.

This lasted until the Fall when Lanlan started school. One morning, to Colonel Ma's surprise, the backyard garden was gone. The fence, the shed, the corn, the vegetables had all vanished. Something else was missing. Following the same path he'd taken every morning since he'd first discovered the garden, Colonel Ma walked to the bank of the quiet moat. It was still dark, and the early Fall mist hadn't yet started to lift from the still surface of the water. Slowly, a bamboo shoulder pole and a pair of metal pails became visible on the ground at the edge of the water.

Colonel Ma's father had decided to return to his home village. The Colonel and his wife couldn't persuade him to stay. His reason was simple and compelling.

"I belong to our home village and that's where I want to die and be buried," said Colonel Ma's father.

Only years later, after Colonel Ma's father had passed away, did the Colonel realize that his father had bought his own coffin. From Lanlan, he learned that the money had come from the trash that his father had collected and sold.

Colonel Ma did eventually resume his old routine, but with one change. After ten every night, he would spend a few minutes in the room where his father had stayed. It was kept the way his father had left it, except for the bamboo shoulder pole and the pair of metal pails.

BIRDS & BEES IN BEIJING

"You little perverts," laughed Tian Dashan. With shaved head and small eyes, thirteen-year-old Dashan stood, legs apart, in front of the crowd of boys who'd gathered like mosquitoes in front of a concrete apartment building in the State Council's 400 family residential compound in Beijing. It was a cool, September evening in the early 60s. Dashan leered. "You bunch of babies. You want to know about girls, don't you?" Someone begged Dashan to tell them about a game he'd played with the Liu brothers' sister some time ago.

Drawing near the mesmerized crowd, Han Jiang noticed that his good friends, Tian San and Xiao Wu, had begun to pull away. Du Wen trotted after them. Han Jiang followed his three silent friends to their usual meeting place -- the compound's courtyard surrounded by three red brick buildings that made up the compound's inner sanctum. Tian San was in a dudgeon over the behavior of Dashan, his older brother. He and Xiao Wu sat down on the tall, cement border of a large, circular flower bed filled with scarlet coxcombs. Each boy wore the red scarf of a Young Pioneer.

"Don't be upset," said Han Jiang, sitting down on the other side of Tian San. Beside Tian San, Han Jiang looked short and skinny. "We all know you're not at all like your brother. Anyway, everyone in the compound knows that he and the Liu girl played doctor."

"He should be ashamed of himself, examining girls and then bragging about it," said Tian San. His voice trembled.

Du Wen stood in front of the others with his hands on his hips and his round body almost bursting out of his white cotton shirt like a cooked sausage out of its skin. "It's a load of bullshit the way Dashan talks. What does he know about girls? I bet he doesn't even know how he came into this world in the first place."

Han Jiang and his friends stared at Du Wen in surprise. "Do you know?" asked Xiao Wu.

"Of course," said Du Wen. "Don't you know why your parents sleep together in the same bed? They do it to make babies. The more they sleep together, the more babies they make. That's why they always keep us away from the girls." Du Wen looked smugly at his friends. He had a little double chin, and swaggered like a miniature, high-ranking cadre.

"D'you mean your parents haven't slept together since they made you, Du Wen?" asked Xiao Wu.

Du Wen was puzzled. His freckled face crinkled anxiously.

"Du Wen, if what you say is right," said Han Jiang, "how come Grandpa Meng and Aunty Dai sleep together and they haven't made any babies?"

The other boys stared at each other. They glanced around to make sure that no one else was within ear shot. This was big news. Simultaneously, they moved closer to Han Jiang.

"I've certainly never heard about this before, have you Xiao Wu?" asked Tian San, looking at his friend. There were no secrets between the two. Xiao

Wu shook his head.

"I bet no one else knows about it," said Xiao Wu, looking at Du Wen whose mouth was still hanging open.

"Are you joking, Han Jiang?" asked Du Wen in a low voice.

"Do I look like I'm joking?" asked Han Jiang in a loud whisper. "I saw it with my own eyes one day when I was at Zheng Biao's home. Remember, Zheng Biao's family shares an apartment with Aunty Dai's family. Her bedroom is close to the bathroom. You'd think she'd close the door all the way, but she didn't. On my way to the bathroom, I saw Aunty Dai and Grandpa Meng lying naked together in bed! Grandpa Meng was smoking his pipe, and Aunty Dai was laughing. I told Zheng Biao what I saw. He said they've been like that for a long time."

The four boys relished the moment.

"Well, but they haven't made any babies, have they?" asked Xiao Wu, at last.

"Forget about babies, will you? This is important," said Du Wen, impatiently.

"This involves real people we all know!"

"It's more sickening than my brother's game with that Liu girl. At least they're the same age," said Tian San. He looked as if he'd swallowed toad venom. "How old is Grandpa Meng? Sixty? Maybe older! When did the Red Army start on the Long March?"

"Who knows? Around 1920 or 1930, or maybe it was 1949?" said Xiao Wu.

"I don't think it was 1949," said Du Wen. "That was the year we were liberated."

Who'd need a Long March after Liberation? Get to your point, Tian San. Are you saying because Grandpa Meng is sixty years old, he shouldn't sleep with Aunty Dai?"

"I wonder how old Aunty Dai is?" asked Xiao Wu.

"Her two daughters are still in kindergarten," said Han Jiang, "which means she could be younger than my Mom. Maybe around thirty at most."

"All I'm saying is, why should a much older man -- he's a grandpa -- sleep with an aunt like Aunty Dai who's so much younger? It doesn't make any sense, does it?" asked Tian San.

"It makes a lot of sense," said Xiao Wu. "Aunty Dai's husband is working in the embassy in North Korea. He only comes back at the end of each year. If Aunty Dai's two daughters are in kindergarten, she must be awfully lonely. Why shouldn't Grandpa Meng keep Aunty Dai company?"

"Still they don't have to be stark naked in bed together, do they?" said Du Wen. "Somehow, it doesn't sound right. Grandpa Meng has his own family. Aunty Dai has hers, too. They're not married to each other."

"I was so embarrassed," said Han Jiang. "But it really wasn't my fault, was it? I mean they didn't close their door, and I was there by accident. Right?" Han Jiang looked around at his three friends. They all nodded. "Now, I think they should feel ashamed. Don't people say Grandpa Meng used to be one of Chairman Mao's stretcher bearers during the Long March? Every year Grandpa Meng shows us kids a letter from Chairman Mao with the Chairman's signature on it." Han Jiang kicked the cement border of the flower bed with his heels. "I wonder what Uncle Dai would do if he knew."

"He'd thank Grandpa Meng, of course," said Xiao Wu, "for taking care of Aunty Dai."

"Oh, grow up, Xiao Wu. We're not talking about taking care of people. We're talking about an old man sleeping naked with a young aunty," said Du Wen.

"We're not getting anywhere talking this way," said Han Jiang. "I think we should all go home. Tomorrow we have school."

The four boys finally dragged themselves from the courtyard back to their homes. The crowd they'd left hours ago had diminished in size but was still hovering about in the same place. It was almost time for bed.

As they approached, they heard Tian Dashan's voice. "Wait till you guys hear this story. Then you'll know what you've missed." Tian Dashan had his hands on his hips and was bragging. "One of my classmates from the Municipal Council's residential compound told me a real story that happened in his compound. There was a newlywed couple. They didn't know what to do the first night they slept together. They got locked together. Later, their parents had to call an ambulance to take them to the hospital. They were carried in on the same stretcher and had to be separated surgically on the operation table." All the boys crowed with delight.

"That's the most gross, disgusting thing I've ever heard in my life," said Tian San in a low voice to his friends.

"If what Dashan says is true," said Xiao Wu, "who'd ever want to get married?"

"I think he made it up," said Du Wen.

"I think Du Wen's right. They've got nothing to do, so they've started to make things up," said Han Jiang.

"What happened afterwards, Dashan?" shouted someone in the crowd. "Did they get locked together, again? Or didn't they dare sleep together, again?"

"Don't ask me. How should I know, you nosy rascal?" said Dashan.

"You'd better ask your classmate tomorrow and get an update," said someone else. The crowd agreed boisterously.

"I don't believe a word you're saying, Dashan,"

shouted Du Wen. "How can people get locked together. That doesn't make any sense, does it? Why haven't we heard about anyone getting locked together in our compound? And our compound is three times as big as the Municipal Council's."

"What do you know about anatomy, Du Wen?" asked Tian Dashan. "I bet you don't even know your own sex."

Deeply humiliated, Du Wen started to cry.

"You guys are really limited," said Han Jiang, coming to Du Wen's rescue. "Really stupid."

"I'm going to tell Mom what you said to my friend tonight," said Tian San. "I'm going to tell Mom everything you said."

"You little brat," said Tian Dashan. "You guys are just a bunch of babies." He squinted at his little brother. "You tell Mom, Tian San, and I'll tan your hide."

That night, the four boys secretly rummaged their parents' bookshelves until they found a copy of *The Handbook for Common Medical Knowledge in the Rural Areas*. The book was as common and accessible, then, as Chairman Mao's works in later times. Each boy leafed through the thick volume of closely printed text crammed with detailed drawings intended to help the rural clinic doctor. At the sections on anatomy and gynecology, each boy began carefully to study the pages.

The next day, after dinner, the four boys converged on the courtyard as if by prior agreement. Again, they sat along the concrete edge of the flower bed. They kept silent on the subject for a while, until Tian San could no longer stand it.

"The more I think about yesterday's subject, the more disgusting I think it is," said Tian San.

"Me too," said Xiao Wu. "I didn't know that we're so different from girls. I thought it was just the clothes and games and their pigtails."

"Oh, I knew about it all a long time ago," lied Du Wen.

"It's just terrible to think of that picture in the book and Grandpa Meng and Aunty Dai," said Tian San. "It makes me sick just thinking about it."

"I had an awful day at school." said Han Jiang. "I felt I couldn't talk to girls anymore."

"I had a dream last night," said Du Wen.

"About Grandpa Meng and Aunty Dai. They had a baby at the hospital. And then when they came out, they were arrested." The boys were silent for a moment.

"I don't ever want to get married," said Xiao Wu.

Du Wen stood up, put his hands on his hips and stuck out his belly. "Whoever gets married is a turtle's egg!"

"Agreed, everyone?" asked Tian San.

"Agreed!"

The boys felt like the heroes of the Peach Garden meeting in *The Romance of the Three Kingdoms*, even though they didn't seal their pact with blood.

"O.K.," said Han Jiang. "Now, let's play 'catch the spy.'"

The Bridge

"Don't we all belong to Guofu Dayuan?" cried a voice in the center of the crowd of mainly elementary school boys who had gathered inside the gate of Guofu Dayuan, the residential Quad belonging to the State Council in Beijing in the 1960s.

Han Jiang, being short and skinny, had to elbow his way from the periphery to the center to see what was going on. From a gap in the crowd, he caught sight of an agitated Zhou Wei shouting in the center. Zhou Wei was thirteen, two years Han Jiang's senior. Zhou Wei's usually handsome face was purple from shouting, and his voice was hoarse. Sweat soaked the hair on his forehead and darkened the collar of his short-sleeved, blue athletic shirt.

"Look what they've done to my arms and trousers! Are we going to let those fucking bastards across the bridge bully us again?" asked Zhou Wei.

"No!" roared the crowd.

Han Jiang squeezed his head up against someone's shoulder to get a better look. He saw that Zhou Wei's arms were covered with bruises, dirt and blood and that one leg of his new green trousers was torn from the bottom up to the knees.

"Get your sweaty head away from me," grunted the boy against whom Han Jiang was squeezing himself. The boy turned his head, and Han Jiang recognized Tian San's freckled, baby face. Though they were the same age, Tian San was a little taller.

"What's going on?" asked Han Jiang. "How come Zhou Wei got beaten up?"

"It's so exciting!" said Tian San when he recognized his friend. "It looks like there's going to be a real fight this time!"

Among the crowd, Han Jiang saw his friends Xiao Wu and Du Wen. On the other side of the crowd, he saw his brother, Han Chuan, and Tian San's brother, Tian Dashan, and the stalwart Zheng Biao.

The crowd was getting thicker and more reckless. The latecomers cursed and shouted. Like

Han Jiang, they'd caught only a few words from Zhou Wei, but the sight of the blood and torn trousers stirred them in a way that surprised Han Jiang.

"Just show us who did it, Zhou Wei," shouted Zheng Biao. "We'll fix them!" Zheng Biao, who was thirteen, was tall and sturdy. He began rolling up his sleeves.

"Let's go! Let's get 'em!" The words rolled like low thunder through the crowd.

Before Han Jiang realized what was happening, he found himself being carried along by the crowd which surged out of the compound gate. They ran in the direction of the bridge, a couple of hundred yards south of the compound.

The next day, as Han Jiang stepped into the noisy classroom and walked to his desk at the front of the room, he noticed that the room had suddenly grown quiet. The whole morning, Han Jiang felt cold stares boring through the back of his skull. Not even one classmate greeted him during the ten-minute breaks between classes. After school, on the way out of the schoolyard, he caught up with his best friend, Wu Zhongyi.

"Zhongyi, what's the matter?" asked Han Jiang. "Why did everyone treat me like I had the measles? What did I do?"

Zhongyi, short and stocky, kept walking ahead, as if he hadn't heard Han Jiang.

"Wait, Zhongyi. I don't care about the others! But aren't you my friend?"

Zhongyi stopped in his tracks. "You ought to know the answer yourself. You probably think we didn't see you in the fight yesterday, don't you? Shame on you," said Zhongyi.

"What? I was only a bystander," said Han Jiang.

"A bystander? You were running and shouting with the crowd and throwing stones at us. Some bystander. Just because that fucking Quad is for big shots, d'you think you can do whatever you want and get away with it by hiding in the crowd?"

"But you guys beat up the guy from our compound, first," said Han Jiang.

"So now it's 'us' against 'you' is it? I thought you said we were friends," said Zhongyi. "You joined the fight without even getting the facts straight. Double shame on you!" Zhongyi spat on the ground and resumed his walk without looking back at Han Jiang. •

Han Jiang watched his best friend disappear around a corner. All he could remember about yesterday's fight was his running with the crowd. He couldn't remember throwing stones. Bicycle bells tinkled behind him. He found that he was standing in the middle of the narrow lane outside the school. The school door was closed for lunch, and the area looked deserted. He kicked the dust on the sidewalk as he walked slowly toward the bridge. On the other side of the bridge was the State Council's residential compound, his home, the Quad.

On the bridge, Han Jiang looked down over the concrete balustrade at the water in the moat. He remembered the first time he'd crossed it four years ago. The bridge had been made of wooden planks, then. The planks had squeaked under his feet, and he could see, between the almost foot-sized gaps, the eerie, dark green water far below.

Frequent crossings, however, had gradually

worn away his fear. And then, one day, the wooden bridge was gone. Months later, in time for Han Jiang's second year at elementary school, a cement bridge was constructed in its place. For Han Jiang, it was never quite the same, again. The Chinese word for bridge, qiao, with "wood" as a part of the written character, had lost its meaning. Without the wood, it was no longer a bridge.

By parental decision, Han Jiang and his older brother, Han Chuan, attended the school across the bridge since it was closest to the Quad. The other children living in the Quad all went to various schools in Beijing's Western District. Han Jiang's school, however, was in a different district, where the residents were mostly workers rather than cadres. The two districts were separated by the moat and connected only by the bridge.

Han Jiang remembered his first day at school. Han Chuan had led him by the hand, across the bridge, to the school. The school didn't look much like one. Going up the big, worn-out stone steps, and crossing the high wooden threshold with its two thick wood doors painted a dull red, Han Jiang had found himself standing in a yard. On one side was the city wall and, on the other sides, were low, grey brick buildings with grey, tiled roofs, large wood columns and window frames of carved wood. The school was a revamped Buddhist monastery.

Han Jiang had made friends quickly. Wu Zhongyi was the first to invite him to his home. Zhongyi's father worked in a steel factory and his mother worked on the assembly line at a biscuit factory. Zhongyi had two younger sisters. He and his sisters took care of all the household chores, including washing, cooking and cleaning.

The whole family lived in a one-room shanty in a courtyard shared by eight families. Zhongyi's two sisters slept in an ingeniously constructed, cascade-like series of beds which were built like a chest of drawers opening from the side. Zhongyi slept on a separate plank, while his parents slept on a board only a little wider than a twin-sized bed. The beds did double service, of course, as chairs. When Zhongyi's father returned from work at night, he hung his bicycle on the wall near the door.

The family shared an outdoor cold water tap

with the other seven families in the same yard, and everyone used the public toilets around the street corner. Zhongyi's father had built a little room, just outside the window, where they cooked their meals on a coal burner. The window served as a convenient outlet to pass food and dishes in and out. Once the dining table was set up, the door was blocked, and the room was full.

As Han Jiang began to make more friends at school, he found that many of his classmates lived in similar circumstances. He enjoyed their hospitality, too. He especially liked the fresh, steamed bread and noodles, made from scratch, by Zhongyi and his sisters. After school, instead of going straight home, Han Jiang liked to hang out with Zhongyi, carefully working the dump site near their home and fighting crowds of other kids for half-burnt coals and wood shavings discarded by a nearby furniture workshop and a vinegar factory.

"Han Jiang! Do you know what time it is now? Don't you want to eat your lunch?" Han Jiang was suddenly aroused from his thoughts by his brother's voice.

"Hurry up! Ten more minutes, and the dining hall will be closed," shouted Han Chuan from the other end of the bridge. Reluctantly, Han Jiang made his way back to the Quad.

At the entrance to the dining hall, he was blocked by a group of youngsters headed by Zhou Wei.

"Han Jiang, it's time for you to donate your food tickets for the defense of our compound," said Zhou Wei with a grin.

"I don't owe any of you favors," said Han Jiang. "Why should I give you my tickets?" Out of the corner of his eyes, he saw that Zhou Wei's cohorts had surrounded him on all sides. He knew they were waiting for a signal from Zhou Wei.

"Hey! What's going on there?" called a familiar voice from a distance. It was Zheng Biao. He was the same age as Zhou Wei, but two inches taller and twenty pounds heavier. Han Jiang's eyes brightened. He was saved. He shouted, "Brother Zheng! They won't let me into the dining hall. They're trying to make me give up my food tickets!"

Zhou Wei's crowd melted away with surprising

speed. When Zheng Biao arrived at the dining hall, Zhou Wei was nowhere to be seen.

"What a bunch of chickens -- to bully the little ones," said Zheng Biao, fuming.

Han Jiang rushed into the dining hall and got some less-than-warm rice with fried tomatoes and eggs. It was the tomato season, and Han Jiang noticed that his dish was big on tomatoes and little on eggs. Still, the portion was large, as usual.

Like many of the other children in the Quad, Han Jiang and his brother ate at the dining hall because their parents had been sent to other parts of the country to carry out Party policies and oversee political movements. The Quad's dining hall had been set up to meet the needs of such children. The dining hall also made certain that they had boiled water to drink. Children from the higher-ranking cadre families living in the same compound, however, ate mainly at school or at home where either mothers or nannies did the cooking. Lack of good food, therefore, wasn't the reason for the highway robbery of food tickets.

That evening, at dinner, Han Jiang found his

brother eating with a group of kids at a table in the dining hall. The moment Han Chuan saw him, he called out, "Come over here Han Jiang. I heard that Zhou Wei gave you some trouble at lunch time. Is that true?" Han Jiang reluctantly nodded his head.

"What an ungrateful bastard he is!" said Han Chuan. He then turned to his friends at the table and said, "Didn't we all fight for him yesterday? Now he turns around and bullies my kid brother. Is that fair?"

"Zhou Wei got beaten up because he was taking advantage of some tricyclist," said someone at the table. "The guys on the other side of the bridge saw him hanging on to the back of a cart. It was completely loaded with coals, and the tricycle was pulling it over the bridge. If you ask me, Zhou Wei got what he deserved."

Han Chuan flushed. He stood up and called to his friend, Zheng Biao, who was eating at another table across the hall.

"Zheng Biao! You got to hear this. We've been cheated by Zhou Wei again. That sonofabitch did something shameless outside the compound. That's why he got beaten up. Then he came back and told us a lie. And after all the help we gave him, he's had the nerve to bully my kid brother."

Upon hearing this, the children in the dining hall, about one hundred, became agitated. Some had just been victims of Zhou Wei's assaults. Zheng Biao was hit hardest by the news, because he'd led yesterday's fight. Without saying a word, he pushed aside his food, motioned to his friends and walked out of the dining hall. Han Chuan and Han Jiang followed behind him, along with many of the other children. The crowd moved swiftly to the inner quarters of the Quad where Zhou Wei's family lived.

The inner quarters were one of three distinctive living quarters in the Quad. The other two were the northwest and the southeast quarters both of which were L-shaped, and surrounded the inner quarters on all four sides, turning the Quad into an impenetrable, quadrilateral citadel. On the west side there was one tunnel-like gateway opening onto the main street, and on the east side, a back door hidden behind a courtyard.

The inner quarters consisted of three red-brick

buildings of three stories high. They had large, impressive cement balconies, carved and painted green eaves and sloping, golden-tiled roofs. The three buildings faced a center court where there was a well-tended, long, oblong flower bed as well as a big, circular flower bed with a cement border and a fountain in the center. The Quad had its own gardener and greenhouse. The residents of the inner quarters were mostly the families of deputy ministers or bureau chiefs. They had their own cars, chauffeurs, and secretaries. Their five room apartments came furnished with the comforts of life, including private telephones and T.V.s. They had their own private kitchens and bathrooms with bathtub, and each apartment had two balconies, or a small, private garden if it was on the first floor. The wooden floors were waxed, polished and carpeted.

Zhou Wei's family lived in a first-floor apartment in the inner quarters. As soon as the crowd, led by Zheng Biao, got to the private garden, they started to shout over the fence, calling Zhou Wei to come out. The screen door facing the garden opened slowly.

Zhou Wei's father stepped out. He was a bald-headed Major, an army veteran, and was now serving as the bureau chief of Agricultural Affairs under the State Council.

"What's going on here?" asked Major Zhou. "What did Little Wei do to have all of you come here and shout at us?" Loud complaints flew at the Major. Upon hearing what his son had done both inside and outside the compound, the Major ordered Zhou Wei to come out. As Zhou Wei came through the screen door, silence fell over the crowd. In an instant, Zhou Wei's father, standing in the little garden behind the fence, had pulled out the dark brown, leather belt from around his waist, grabbed his son and begun whipping him. Zhou Wei screamed, but his father's grip was relentless. The crowd immediately dispersed.

When Han Jiang returned to the southeast quarters where he lived, his ears were still ringing with Zhou Wei's screams. It was already dark, and the Quad was only dimly lit. Looking up at the window of his own apartment on the third floor, Han Jiang realized that Han Chuan hadn't come home yet. He sat down near the hallway to wait for him.

For a moment, Han Jiang felt sorry for Zhou Wei who'd been such a source of envy to him. The first time he'd visited Zhou Wei, who actually had his own private bedroom, he'd been amazed by the trunkful of hard-to-get items that Zhou Wei owned -- expensive cigarette cases his father had saved for him, a mahogany carom set, an ivory set of checkers, and a miniature electric railway system with automatic controls, a gift from his father's friend who was a high-ranking diplomat in Moscow. For days after, Han Jiang had dreamt about owning some of those things.

"The water's ready!" said someone, shouting in the distance from the direction of the dining hall. Han Jiang knew, then, that it was nine o'clock and time for the dining hall staff to bring steaming, boiled water in big kettles for children like him, whose parents were away. He stood up quickly, straining his eyes to catch sight of the water-bearer in the darkness. Someone ran towards his building. Before he could tell who, that person had slipped and fallen, hitting the ground with a loud thud. As

Han Jiang ran up to him, he found Han Chuan lying on the ground, blood pouring out from the back of his head.

Han Chuan was rushed to the Children's Hospital. He'd had a concussion and had received emergency treatment including several stitches to his head and a shot of antibiotics. Because of the severity of his injury, Han Chuan stayed in the hospital for a week. Later, he told Han Jiang that he'd failed to see someone's clothesline fastened between the trees as he was running in the dark. When he fell backwards, his head had hit a brick curb.

The rupture between Han Jiang and his school friends slowly healed. But Wu Zhongyi still took it hard and refused to befriend Han Jiang again. One afternoon, after school, when Han Jiang was halfway across the bridge, he heard someone calling him from behind. He turned around and saw Zhongyi standing at the end of the bridge. The two hurried towards each other.

"I heard that your brother got hurt in the head," said Zhongyi. "My whole family was sorry to hear about it. My sisters and I made some noodles for him, and for you. I can't go into your compound. You have to cook them yourself." Zhongyi pulled out a package, wrapped in newspaper, from his schoolbag, and handed it to Han Jiang.

"Why can't you come to our compound, Zhongyi?" asked Han Jiang as he took the large package. The fight was a thing of the past.

"Never mind why, Han Jiang. Say hello to your brother for us," said Zhongyi. "And take care of yourself, too." Turning around, Zhongyi walked back towards his side of the bridge.

Through the newspaper wrapping, Han Jiang could feel the soft, homemade noodles inside. He could almost see Zhongyi and his two sisters working at the family table, mixing and kneading flour, rolling it out, folding it and slicing it into thin noodles for him and Han Chuan. He couldn't understand why Zhongyi had said he couldn't come to the compound. In fact, Han Jiang suddenly realized, Zhongyi had never come to the State Council's residential compound even when they were best friends. Standing on the bridge, squeezing the soft noodles in their wrapping, Han Jiang looked to one end and then to the other end of the bridge. Slowly, he started walking home towards the Quad.

THE BALCONY

I like sitting here looking at the sunrise and sunset, the moon and the stars. I used to like looking at other things too. Like the grey city walls out there and a footpath down here. But one day they were gone. There were tiled roofs and a noisy street. I used to like looking at people as well. Big people, little people with black hair, white hair and no hair. But they changed too, faster than the city walls and the footpath. They smiled at me.

Then one day they started to make faces at me and yell "Idiot!" I don't know why. I sit here all by myself. I don't bother anyone. That's when I started to close my eyes. I could still see things. I saw people, small like spiders, climbing the city walls, and boys and girls like ducks chasing after flying things in the grass down that path. They were running, laughing, out of breath. They wore red scarves around their white collars. I saw a tiny curly green vine hanging over the edge of a balcony above my head like a hanging ghost. I smelt the flowers.

Then I woke up and something smelt like my own pee and I heard giggles upstairs. I opened my eyes and saw trickles of water flowing down from the balcony above my head. I heard Xiao Du's nanny shouting from below. *Look what you've done to my flowers. You rascals! Don't you think you can fool me this time.*

I pushed my head out between the iron-bars around my balcony and looked down. There was nothing. Nothing wrong at all. But at night, it was dark. I heard loud noises from upstairs.

Whose idea was this? Peeing on people's flowers. You shameless wretches. Who did it? Answer me. Uncle Tian's voice was very loud.

Look how angry your papa is. You'd better tell him straight and apologize to Xiao Du's nanny. I heard Aunty Li's voice.

It's not going to be that easy this time. Ever since Grandma left, they've been causing trouble for me in the compound. Raising hell in the dining hall, robbing other little kids of their food tickets and now peeing from the balcony. I've had enough of them this time. Dashan, you come over here! I heard a slapping sound and a scream.

You're the oldest. You should've known better, you shameless thing. Uncle Tian's voice was like knives. I heard whipping sounds. Dashan was screeching, so were his brothers.

Lao Tian, Lao Tian. They shouldn't have done what they did but they're still young, said Aunty Li.

Young? When I was their age, I had to work in the fields for a living. Now they've got everything, and they've started acting like those damn rich landlord's kids in the village. Is that what we fought for? I won't have it. The whipping never stopped.

Stop it, Lao Tian. Look how sorry they are. We shouldn't have let Grandma leave us in the first place. Aunty Li was crying. There was still whipping. The boys were still crying.

I put both my hands to my ears. But I could still hear things. I heard Dashan's Grandma's voice. She was telling a story upstairs. *One day a farmer saw a little worm in his field. He didn't think much of it and walked away. The next day, he came upon the same little worm in his field, he picked it up and threw it away. The third day, he saw the worm in his field again. He thought to himself, 'I am going to kill it.' That very moment, the worm started to grow. It grew longer and longer, and it grew into a humongous size. The farmer was scared and started to run. He ran and ran and out of the corner of his eyes, he saw the worm was running after him. Out of breath, he passed out. When he woke up, he discovered the little worm was lying in his hand.*

Knowing it could change its shape, the farmer didn't know what to do with it...

When Grandma Tian came to live with Dashan and his two little brothers, they sounded like chirping sparrows. They called Grandma this and Grandma that day in and day out. I wished I could be upstairs. I heard a lot of watering going on but saw no trickles. Until one day I saw a tiny curly green vine hanging from the edge of their balcony like a hanging-ghost. I smelt the flowers.

One morning, I heard the tiny sounds. Dashan shouted in the balcony, Grandma, Grandma, they've hatched! Look at them. They're so furry and cute. I heard kissing sounds. I was the first to hear them, I wanted to say.

Then one day, I heard Dashan and his brothers calling Grandma from downstairs.

After that, I saw a basket with a rope attached to it coming down slowly from the balcony above, right in front of my eyes. I could hear the sounds inside the basket. It was covered tightly with a piece of cloth. I never allowed my eyes to blink for a second until that basket was on the ground. Dashan pulled off the cloth. Chicks and ducklings ran everywhere, on the path, in the grass.

Every afternoon, Dashan and his brothers called Grandma to let down the basket. They called her for other things as well, money to buy popsicles, chestnuts roasted with sugar and baked sweet potatoes. Every time they asked, a paper ball flew down from the balcony above. And one day she was gone.

After Dashan and his brothers got beaten, their whole family moved out of the apartment above us and into the one on the second floor where there was no balcony. I could still see Dashan and his brothers when they put their heads out of their windows. Their heads were shaved now, and people started to call them monks.

That's when they started to make faces at me and yell "Idiot!" Those puny boys and girls on the path. I never look at them!

I was woken up by the sounds of many, many footsteps in the early morning. One, two, one. One, two, one. I smelt the dust. The path below my balcony was filled with a cloud of moving green, green hats, green jackets, green trousers and green shoes. Then came big green trucks. The green grass was gone. I felt the shudders. I could hardly breath.

What's going on out there, Lao Tang, Mother's voice came through the screen door of my balcony.

Didn't they say something about building a subway under those city walls, Wen Lan? They must have started now, Father said.

Well, I guess that's the end of our peace and quiet for a while. It's too bad, too.

The city walls are part of Beijing's history, said Mother.

One day, I saw a limp-duck disappear under

one big green truck. It appeared again, smashed. I smelt the dust.

The driver was grinning at me from his seat with a cigarette hanging from his mouth. He was wearing a blue jacket and a dusty basket helmet. I looked at the squashed duck. It wasn't there anymore.

I thought they'd finished their job, Lao Tang? How come they're back again,

Mother's voice came through the screen door again.

Oh, no. They're far from finished, Wen Lan. They've just started. The construction soldiers have torn down the walls, removed the debris, and gone back to where they came from. Now the workers have moved in for the real job, Father said.

I was woken up by a scream. Some people were laughing somewhere below my balcony. I tried to stick my head out between the iron bars. I saw a truck speed away in a cloud of dust. I smelt the gas.

Bravo! Dashan. You got him right through his hand on the wheel. Wasn't that something, guys, I heard a boy's voice. People were clapping, whistling and shouting.

Superb shot. No doubt about it, another voice said.

I looked down from my balcony and saw something like a cigarette butt tossed out of one window on the second floor on the left. The noise came from there.

I looked around. The balcony was empty. Through the iron bars, I saw the walls were gone. I started to cry.

Shut up, you idiot! You want to be shot too? I hear you one more time, you're dead. D'you hear me? A shaved head of a big boy looked at me out of the second-floor window. He waved something in his hand up at me.

Leave him alone Dashan. He doesn't know nothing, someone said.

I don't know about that. He's an idiot, all right. It's bad luck. It's disgusting to hear him growling on that fuckin' balcony.

I heard the rumbles of trucks coming my way. I saw the cloud and truckloads of blue jackets with basket helmets. I smelt the gas and dust. The trucks stopped. Blue jackets with steel bars and shovels were jumping out of the trucks and running on foot everywhere. They were shouting and throwing stones at the window on the second floor. They ran into the building.

Suddenly, something, a long, bundle of straw tied with ropes, was thrown out of the window. It landed on the floor of one of the trucks. It sounded heavy. Blue jackets climbed back into the trucks and engines started to roar. With cloud and noise, they moved away.

Late at night, it was very dark. There were stars. I heard whispering sounds through the screen door.

They could have flown Lao Tian back from Canton, couldn't they? Mother asked.

That would've been too late and wouldn't have saved Dashan's life either. When Premier Zhou arrived at the construction site this afternoon, they'd tied Dashan to a post. They were ready to let that injured worker shoot Dashan one hundred times, using the same air gun within the same distance, said Father.

How terrible! But I wonder why Premier Zhou himself had to go this time, said Mother.

Who else could stop them? Think about it. There were hundreds and thousands of workers around the site. They wanted to kill Dashan, said Father.

I wonder what went wrong with those kids. They used to be so nice. Were they out of their minds? Shooting people with their air guns. What would happen if they were to get real guns! Mother started to cry.

I didn't see Dashan and his brothers anymore. One day I saw strange faces popping out of the windows on the second floor.

I heard Lao Tian's family has moved away, said Mother.

The place must have too many bad memories for Lao Tian. Luckily, he got Dashan out of police custody and into the People's Liberation Army in Xinjiang, said Father.

Then it started to rain. The sun, the moon and the stars were all gone. I started to scratch at the screen door on my balcony. I wanted to go inside.

THE JAUNDICE WARD

"Sailing the seas depends on the helmsman,
Life and growth depend on the sun,
Rain and dew drops nourish the crops,
Making revolution depends on Mao Tsetung Thought."

Han Jiang was awakened by the blast of the loudspeaker through the closed window. He opened his eyes and searched the room for a clock. It was still dark outside, but he could hear someone snoring in the same room. He touched the rough, cotton cover of his quilt, the pillowcase, the sheet, and the pajamas on his body. Since when had he started to wear pajamas? He was puzzled. He was glad, though, that the protean reptile he'd been fleeing moments ago was only a nightmare. That didn't mean he wasn't afraid, for he knew very well that it took only changing shapes and disguises to make a real monster. He was sorry, now, that he'd listened to so many stories about reptiles. At nine years of age, he began to think, he should've been past such stories. Everything in the room seemed to be camouflaged. Objects under the chair reminded him of salamanders under rocks. Even the slippers on the floor looked like hermit crabs, not to mention those pale, fish-like things hanging near the sink in one corner of the room. Everything was in flux nowadays, he reasoned. Shapes and colors that were only too obvious and familiar were all the scarier because of their sneaky ability to change.

The room reeked of disinfectant. Gradually, as the sky began to lighten outside the window, Han Jiang saw another bed, parallel to his, up against the opposite whitewashed wall. The snoring came from the heap under the white quilt on that bed. He began to remember that, only yesterday, he'd been admitted into this room in the Beijing Second Hospital for Contagious Diseases as a jaundice-hepatitis patient. His brother, Han Chuan, had just spent a month in this same room. He'd been released a

week ago. Han Chuan's roommate, then, was

Cao Bao, and now Han Jiang had inherited him. Short and fat, with a round face, Cao Bao was also nine. He'd been in this isolation ward more than a month, and he'd said he was going to leave soon.

"Fish can't leave the water, nor melons leave the vine,

The revolutionary masses can't live without the Communist Party,

Mao Tsetung Thought is the sun that never sets."

Loud voices upstairs were singing along with the song that boomed over the loudspeaker. People were pounding their feet rhythmically against the floor, following the catchy tune. Han Jiang's roommate was awakened by the sound. He kicked his quilt off the bed and rubbed his eyes.

'What's going on up there? An earthquake or something?" shouted Cao Bao. "Don't they want me to get well? Or what? It's a conspiracy to keep me locked up in this fuckin' hospital!" He looked around the room and found Han Jiang staring at him.

"Hey! What're you staring at?"

"Nothing. I don't know. I'm your roommate," said Han Jiang.

"I'm not that dumb, partner," said Cao Bao, sitting up at the edge of his bed. "I know who you are. Your brother bragged a lot about you. I didn't realize he was lying, though, till yesterday when you came in. Oh, my. You were some sight, all right. But not what I'd had in mind. A bag of bones is what you are. You'll never make it, I tell you. Not a chance in a thousand years." Cao Bao shook his head like a doctor.

People were starting to move around upstairs, in the adjacent rooms and in the hallway. The isolation wards were awake. Han Jiang slowly got off his bed and moved weakly to the sink. He'd lost weight and grown thinner than ever. He'd lost his appetite as well. Whatever he ate, he threw up sooner or later. When he was diagnosed with jaundice-hepatitis, he was admitted into the hospital right away.

"Not so fast, partner," said Cao Bao from his bed. "You can't use the sink in this room. I run things here."

Han Jiang stopped halfway to the sink. He was sorry he'd tried to stand up in the first place. Dragging himself back to the bed required a big effort.

"Cao Bao," said Han Jiang, as he turned around. "Let's make a deal. There're only two of us in this room. I'll try my best not to get in your way, and you do the same for me, O.K.?"

"No way," said Cao Bao. "I don't want your germs around. I don't want to die with you in this room. You use the sink in the bathroom across the hallway, you hear me?"

Han Jiang dragged himself towards the door. He felt dizzy, and he could only move by supporting himself against the wall. Once in the hallway, he was surprised to see slogans, written on what seemed like endless rolls of toilet paper, covering the walls.

Down with the Reactionary Bourgeois Medical Authorities!

Set the Isolation Wards free from Reactionary Bureaucrats!

Freedom! Not Isolation!

Revolutionary Spirits Can Never Be Confined!

Long Live the Great Proletarian Cultural Revolution!

The movement had just started outside the hospital. Han Jiang was surprised that it'd caught on so quickly here, at the hospital, where he'd least expected it. Not that he didn't like it. He'd been very active in the movement at school when it started. In fact, he'd been so active that when he realized he'd caught this acute, infectious disease and had to be hospitalized, he'd felt extremely disappointed in himself.

The sink in the public bathroom was plugged with toilet paper. The bathroom itself was a mess. Han Jiang had to return to his room. The hallway grew noisier and more crowded. Young patients about Han Jiang's age were reading and commenting on the slogans on the walls. Han Jiang caught sight of Cao Bao's excited, chubby face among the crowd. He was talking quickly, and his audience seemed mesmerized. Han Jiang felt too weak to walk over to the listeners. He took advantage of Cao Bao's absence from the room, and quickly washed his hands and face. In the mirror, he looked at his two sunken eyes and bony cheeks. His skin was an unhealthy yellow, shiny and translucent. He crawled to his bed and lay down.

Han Jiang was later awakened from a doze, this time by shouts coming from the hallway.

"We want decent food! We want to change the rules!" Cao Bao's voice seemed even louder than the rest of the crowd. He seemed to be a natural leader. But why, Han Jiang wondered, had his parents given him a less than glorious name? Cao Bao -- Cao the Treasure -- if pronounced carelessly could easily sound like "bag of straw" or "bumpkin."

That morning, breakfast was delayed by an hour. When it arrived, instead of the rice porridge and steamed bread prescribed by the doctors for the patients in this ward, everyone had soymilk and deep-fried bread. Cao Bao was extremely pleased with himself, for he'd led the protest that morning. The way he hopped back to his room told volumes. For quite some time, he was intoxicated with his first success.

"Hey, partner," said Cao Bao to Han Jiang. "Did you get some of the yummies this morning? If you listen to me, you won't have any trouble here. You'll be able to do and eat whatever you want!" Cao Bao then saw Han Jiang's portion of food on the bedside table. Han Jiang hadn't touched it.

Cao Bao raised his brows and said, "Are you wasting the fruits of our victory? I've been wanting to eat this stuff for ages. Here, you haven't even touched the bread or the soymilk. Who do you think you are? Some sort of prince or aristocrat?" Upon hearing his loud complaints, many patients gathered at the door of the room.

Cao Bao turned to the small crowd of spectators and shouted, "Are we making revolution or not, comrades?"

"Yeah! Yeah! We are! We are!" The crowd responded boisterously.

'Well, comrades. Here we are. We have a real case of counter-revolution. Didn't we fight to have our breakfast menu changed this morning? That's how we got what we wanted. But look here." Cao

Bao turned around to Han Jiang who was still lying in bed and pointed to his untouched food on the bedside table. "He's refused to eat the food we all fought for!"

"Make him get up and eat it!" someone suggested.

"What if he's too sick to eat it?" asked a weak voice. "He just came here yesterday."

"Shut up, Lu Tong!" shouted Cao Bao. "Who needs people like you in the revolution? You can't even tell the difference between friends and enemies."

"Why is he an enemy?" asked Lu Tong, the boy with the weak voice. "Because he's too sick to eat? Don't forget, when you first came in, you were too sick to go to the toilet by yourself."

"Someone get him out of here, will you?" said Cao Bao, but no one listened. Cao Bao grew red with anger.

"You don't want to eat it now? Fine," said Cao Bao, turning again to Han Jiang. "But you're not going to have lunch until you finish this food, d'you hear me?" Cao Bao stalked out of the room with the crowd following on his heels.

Han Jiang felt a momentary nausea. He looked up at the clock on the wall. It was already nine thirty. He should've taken his medication an hour ago. Around ten, a nurse finally walked into the room. She looked vexed and dissatisfied. She brought Han Jiang a little cup of warm water and his pills.

"It's a bad time for everyone," she said quietly. "If you want to get well soon, don't get involved in anything here. Just lie down quietly and take the prescribed medicine and food and eat some sweet things when you can. Nature will take care of the rest, and you'll be fine within a month." After she'd helped Han Jiang with his medicine, the nurse cleared away the food on the bedside table and left the room. Han Jiang felt a little better. He found the warm water very soothing to his throat and stomach. Gradually he closed his eyes and fell asleep.

Around lunch time, Han Jiang woke up again. He hadn't eaten anything that morning and felt both hungry and thirsty. With a feeble hand, he fumbled in the drawer of the bedside table for the candies he'd brought with him to the hospital. They weren't there anymore. Gone also were his apples. He withdrew his hand and gave up the search. Noises came through the door from the hallway.

Han Jiang heard Cao Bao shouting. "We're human beings, not animals! Why can't we go out for a while every day? Even prisoners have that privilege! Who do they think we are? We're revolutionary rebels, are we not, comrades?"

"Yeah! Yeah! Here! Here!" shouted the young crowd.

"On behalf of the patients of the jaundice ward," said Cao Bao, raising his hoarse voice, "I hereby demand that we be freed from this confinement immediately. From now on we only take food and medicine prescribed by our revolutionary-rebel friends. Comrades! We don't want to be poisoned by the reactionary bourgeois medical authorities, do we?"

"No! No! Never!" responded the crowd. "Down with the reactionary bourgeois medical authorities!"

"I hereby declare that our hunger strike has started," said Cao Bao. "We won't eat anything until our demands are fully met!"

The hallway echoed with cheers and the shouting of slogans -- the same slogans that Han Jiang had read earlier on the toilet paper hanging from the walls. This was followed by the singing of Internationale.

"Tis the final struggle,

Let each stand in his place,

The Internationale shall be the human race."

People from upstairs joined in the singing.

Somehow, the usual solemnity of the song was lost, at that particular moment, on Han Jiang. He was much more concerned about the hunger strike. How could he last without eating anything? How could he get better without taking the doctors' prescribed drugs? Han Jiang was scared to speculate any further. For the first time in his life, even though he was a Young Pioneer, he secretly and sincerely wished that the revolution would go somewhere else.

He lay in his bed with both eyes closed. Strangely, Han Jiang felt a sudden surge of strength return to him. He scrambled off the bed, walked swiftly to the door and scanned the hallway. Through the glass window of what used to be an office for the nurses, Han Jiang saw Cao Bao and his supporters ransacking the files. Torn papers and bottles were flying around. Someone even picked up the telephone receiver and spat on it. Han Jiang quickly shut the door and fastened it from the inside. He started searching the room. Pulling open the drawer of Cao Bao's bedside table, he found his fruit drops, toffees and apples. He brought them back to his bed quickly. He gobbled up some candies and a large apple. Within minutes he'd finished his brunch. After drinking some water from the thermos, he unfastened the door, returned to his bed and lay down.

Around one o'clock, the nurse slid into Han Jiang's room with a metal tray containing food. As soon as she came in, she closed the door behind her. While she was placing his rice and tofu on the table, she whispered to Han Jiang.

"Now they've got what they want, except the right to leave the ward. Don't listen to them. They're crazy. They're bored with life. Here's a bottle of pills." The nurse, who was young, took out a small, brown glass bottle from the pocket of her wrinkled, not overly clean, lab coat. "Take them while you can," she said. "Three times a day, two pills at a time. I'm afraid they're not going to let us serve the patients any longer. The whole hospital is said to be under the control of the rebels. But remember to take the medicine and avoid greasy food."

Before Han Jiang had a chance to thank her, the nurse was gone. Looking around the room, Han Jiang found it very hard to find a place to hide the bottle. He knew that without proper medication he couldn't possibly get well. Han Jiang carefully tore open enough of a gap in his pillow, inside the case, and squeezed the bottle in.

Cao Bao came back to the room very late that night. He looked exhausted and pale. Without saying anything to Han Jiang, he went straight to bed and fell asleep as soon as his head touched the pillow. For the first time that day, Han Jiang felt relieved. He'd been preparing for Cao Bao's making a scene once he'd found out Han Jiang had retrieved his candies and apples.

Nothing happened, however, until a week later. When Han Jiang returned to his room from the bathroom, he found that his bed was gone. Gone also were his pillow and everything else that had belonged to him. He was panic stricken. He ran back into the hallway to look for Can Bao. The leader of the rebels was nowhere to be seen. Han Jiang started to walk along the hallway, looking into each room. To his surprise, no one seemed to be around. The whole place looked completely deserted, without a trace of human life. Then, he heard some muffled sounds from the room at the end of the hallway. That was the room where jaundice-hepatitis patients regularly received ultraviolet treatment. Han Jiang knew that the door had to be locked. He placed his ear against the door and heard Cao Bao's voice.

"Take note of this, each of you," said Cao Bao. "I've changed my name to Cao Weibing." Han Jiang could barely contain a laugh. Cao the Treasure had changed his name to Cao the Guard. The new name sounded very much like a "straw-made guard," and Han Jiang couldn't help but think of scarecrows.

"These are revolutionary times," said Cao Bao. 'We have to live and behave like revolutionaries! Among us, some have been playing the game of passive resistance. They've refused to join the revolution. In this matter, there's no middle ground. You're either a friend or an enemy. Minutes ago, I threw out my roommate. He's a typical example of..."

Han Jiang couldn't listen anymore. He had to find his pillow and his medicine. He left the door and began quickly searching each room in the jaundice ward. The rooms smelled bad and looked chaotic. The beddings hadn't been changed for some time. The nurses' office looked as if a Siberian storm had hit it. Finally, Han Jiang found his bedding and belongings in a small utility room at the opposite end of the hallway. The moment his hand touched the bottle in his pillow, Han Jiang nearly wept for joy. He knew that he now had some hope of getting out of the hospital. He was glad that the room was big enough for his bed and table. In his heart, he thanked Cao Bao, now the scarecrow guard, for throwing him out and setting him free from the terrible room they'd shared. He began to realize the irony of one of the slogans Cao Bao and his cohorts often shouted. "Freedom! Not Isolation!" Without isolation, thought Han Jiang, he couldn't have had any freedom.

Two weeks passed. Han Jiang found out that Cao Bao had already moved three times during those weeks. First, he'd moved into the nurses' office. He called it the Headquarters of the Revolutionary Rebels. Cao Bao declared that he was now the elected rebel leader of the jaundice ward. Lu Tong later told Han Jiang that very few patients knew when or where the election had taken place. Anyhow, one day when the patients had gathered in the ultraviolet treatment room, Cao Bao had suddenly announced the results of the so-called election.

A week later, Cao Bao was thrown out of the office by rebels organized mainly by the nurses. He then moved into an activity room formerly reserved for the doctors. Along with him went his appointed lieutenants. After a few days, they were thrown out once again, this time by their opponents among the patients in the same ward. Cao Bao declared, then, that the rebels who were under his leadership had decided to move out of the doctors' room to occupy the morgue in the basement.

Over the loudspeaker in the ward, Cao Bao described the decision as "an important strategic withdrawal from the enemy stronghold."

Cao Bao said, "To carry out a revolution, we must first preserve our revolutionary strength. Now, we've decided to go underground until we're strong enough to deal our enemy a final, decisive blow!"

After Cao Bao and his cohorts had moved to the morgue, the jaundice ward returned to routine. Lu Tong took the opportunity of Cao Bao's absence from the ward to visit Han Jiang in his little utility room. The two became close friends. From Lu Tong, Han Jiang learned that Cao Bao, like himself, had caught jaundice-hepatitis from eating in a dining hall at school. He'd been admitted into the jaundice ward a week earlier than Han Jiang's brother. But, now, after almost two months he was still in the hospital.

"I sort of feel sorry for him sometimes," said

Lu Tong one day. "Cao Bao was almost well a month ago, and then the movement started here. He was dumb enough to refuse the medicine prescribed by the doctors."

"I guess he just got bored with being confined here," said Han Jiang.

"Sometimes I wonder if he's gone a little crazy," said Lu Tong. "He's always been a hard one to deal with, being an only son in his family and all that. But, now, he seems to be out of his mind. What sane person would want to occupy the morgue?" Lu Tong and Han Jiang both shook their heads.

"That's the last place I'd want to go," said Han Jiang. "I hope he doesn't end up staying there forever."

"From the way he's been behaving, he just might not get out of there," said Lu Tong. "Did you hear that Cao Bao tried to go from the morgue up to the meningitis ward on the second floor, this morning?"

"I must've dozed away again. What did he want to do that for? To kill himself as a revolutionary martyr? What good would that do?" asked Han

Jiang.

"He said over the loudspeaker that he wanted to establish revolutionary ties and exchange revolutionary experiences with all the patients, regardless of which ward they're in," said Lu Tong.

A week later, after having spent an entire month in the jaundice ward, Han Jiang was better, and his doctors agreed to let him go home. The night before his departure, Lu Tong came to see Han Jiang for the last time. The two friends were sorry to be parting. Han Jiang took the initiative to cheer his friend up.

"Do exactly what the nurse told me to do, Lu Tong. You'll be out soon. Then we can see each other again, right?"

Lu Tong sighed. "I wish I'd listened to our nurse a lot earlier -- like you. She passed me a bottle of medicine the same time she gave it to you, but I didn't take it as seriously as you until now. But thank goodness, I know what to do now." Lu Tong tried to look upbeat.

The next day, Han Jiang left the hospital with

his parents and his brother, Han Chuan. He was relieved to be out in the warm, summer air and free of the jaundice ward. He noticed, however, that everything had changed. Big character-posters of all sizes and colors hung everywhere, not only in the hallways and corridors, but on the grey brick walls of the courtyard in front of the hospital. Even the entrance was plastered with slogans and posters. The name of the hospital had been changed too. It was now called the Beijing Second Hospital for Revolutionary Rebels. Han Jiang felt a sudden sadness. For the first time he felt genuinely sorry about leaving his former roommate, Cao Bao. That morning, Lu Tong had told him that Cao Bao had caught scarlet fever and dysentery on top of his jaundice-hepatitis and that he'd been rushed out of the morgue on a stretcher and taken to the emergency room.

CHIMERAS

Wu Zhongyi had decided to make a change in his life. He would get his family a new apartment. He'd been married eight years, and even had a seven-year-old daughter, but he still had no place to call his own. What was more, his father had calmly asserted that things would never change. They never had, and never would.

Wu Zhongyi was thirty-two. Before his marriage, he'd lived with his parents and two sisters in a two-room shanty in old Xuanwu District in Beijing. The shanty was one of five that clung to both sides of a narrow, perennially muddy lane leading from a vinegar factory. Squatting almost opposite the factory, it turned the lane into an impromptu courtyard shared by eight families. Both the shanty-courtyard and the vinegar factory went as far back as the latter part of the Qing dynasty.

As soon as Wu Zhongyi and his two younger

sisters were able to talk, they'd complained about the pungent odors from the factory and the residues of fermented sorghum and vinegar yeast dumped right outside the factory, at the edge of the lane, and next to the courtyard. In summer, the acrid mixture rotted in the heat making such a stench that pedestrians avoided the entrance to the lane.

"If your ancestors could stand it, so can you," said Wu Zhongyi's father, a steel worker. "Besides, where else can we go? Don't get any fancy ideas. We've been living here since your great grandpa's time, and no one in this family has ever been able to move out."

Wu Zhongyi's short, heavily built father had unusually swarthy skin, a fleshy face with thick lips, a cauliflower nose and wavy, black hair. For some reason, Zhongyi's once willowy and fair-skinned mother, after years of marriage, had changed into a smaller version of her middle-aged husband. Years later, when Zhongyi and his two sisters turned into almost perfect replicas of their parents, Zhongyi's father had an explanation.

"What's that foreign devil's name who said apes

could become men because of the environment? It won't be long before we all become apes again with all this damned vinegar running around us."

"But why can't we move somewhere else?" asked Wu Zhongyi. Many of his classmates and friends lived under better conditions.

"You wait till you're on your own, my son," answered his father. "Then you'll know why."

Wu Zhongyi's father was right. Once he'd started working, Wu Zhongyi began to see why. Zhongyi was a driver in the steel factory where his father had worked all his life until his recent retirement. For more than a decade, now, Wu Zhongyi had been unable to find a place of his own. For obvious reasons, when he'd gotten married, he'd moved out of the shanty. But, he and his wife, Li Yulan, had had to live separately in their respective factory dormitories which were located on opposite sides of two city districts. The bike ride between the dormitories was at least one and a half hours, in one direction, during the non-rush hours.

That hadn't prevented Zhongyi and Yulan from conceiving their only child, their daughter,

Ying Ying. Wu Zhongyi's five roommates had been kind enough to let him and the bride spend their first two nights in the men's dormitory at the steel factory. After that, the honeymoon was over. Wu Zhongyi and Li Yulan had to meet in weird places and at strange hours. More than once, Wu Zhongyi had been stopped or taken away by the security men in Yulan's textile factory as a night intruder in the women's dormitory. Despite all the difficulties, they'd had Ying Ying. But, like many other "dormitory couples" in Beijing, they had yet to experience one normal day as a married couple.

Once, when Wu Zhongyi had taken Yulan and Ying Ying to visit his parents, he'd complained about the situation. They were sitting around the family's table made of welded, thin steel plates and rods "borrowed" from the factory and covered with a blue plastic tablecloth that had gone yellow and stiff with age.

"Zhongyi," said his father, "didn't I tell you that no one in this family has ever succeeded in moving out of this place? You just never listen." He paused to gulp down tea directly from the spout of the pot.

"You always say that times have changed and we're living in a different society now. I'm not going to argue with you. I don't care what the society's called. The hell with those fancy names! Qing Dynasty, Republic of China and now, People's Republic -- they're all the same! From the Qing Dynasty to now, how many revolutions have we had? And how many people have died in them? Has it ever done us any good? We're still stuck right here, aren't we?"

"There must be some difference, Dad," said Yulan, who'd already begun to look like a smaller version of Wu Zhongyi.

"Oh, I'm not saying there's no difference, Yulan. Like the other day Zhongyi got that speeding ticket driving that fucking truck? Before the Liberation, the cop would've slapped him three times in the face, and that would've been the end of that. But now, look at him. Zhongyi's had to pay out three ten-yuan notes, one third of his entire month's salary, with that ticket! What kind of difference is that?" Despite his anger, Wu Zhongyi's father was pleased with the comparison he'd made. He helped himself to another noisy gulp from the tea pot.

Wu Zhongyi was annoyed. "I'd say there's a big difference between three slaps in the face and a thirty-yuan ticket, Dad. Besides, we should all be a little grateful for what we have. I doubt very much I could've become a truck driver thirty years ago. I might've been out on the streets begging."

"Crap, son. Fucking crap. Your great uncle was a truck driver. Don't give me that crap from the newspapers! The newspapers are the biggest load of crap. I'm not blind or deaf. I'd have been the first to notice any changes if there'd been any. Why should I be grateful? For nothing done for me or us?"

Wu Zhongyi felt a growing irritation. His father continued.

"You want a difference, a real difference, son? Then you got to be really big. Not like your Ma, here. Look at her. She's worked hard for how many years? And handed in how many applications to join the Party? So now, she's finally got herself in. And what's the difference? She's got to pay a two-yuan membership fee every month. You and me - at least we're not Party members. We don't pay anything." Everyone in the family laughed except

Wu Zhongyi's mother.

"Hah! Talk about a sour old man!" she said. "The vinegar around this place has gone to your brains, Lao Wu. Aren't you afraid of poisoning your children, too?"

Wu Zhongyi's father smiled like a brown buddha. "A proletarian cannot possibly poison his working-class offspring. It's a contradiction in terms. All I'm saying is, if you want change, forget it. You have to be someone as big as General Fu Zuoyi. He killed all those Communists, and then, hei! He changed his mind. Just before the Liberation of Beijing, he came over to our side. Smart move. Not only did he get out of being executed, but he's been treated like some dignitary ever since. What's happened to his lieutenants and the soldiers under him? Too bad for them. They haven't been left alone even once in any of these endless movements, have they? If you're not big enough, things'll never get better for you."

Wu Zhongyi came away from his parents' shanty home unconvinced and irate. Yulan and Ying Ying were quiet and seemed depressed. Zhongyi decided, then, it was time to prove his father wrong.

That night, as he lay on an upper bunk bed, in the mid-summer heat, and listened to the roars and wheezes of five co-workers, Wu Zhongyi began to consider his options. He thought of the six years he'd spent in the countryside as one of those "rusticated youths" after high school graduation. That was followed by eight years in the steel factory. What'd he been waiting for? Mao had died; that had made a difference.

Along with other classmates, he'd been able to get out of that poverty-stricken village and return to Beijing. But, to what? To this huge, impersonal steel factory where his father had labored all his life and gotten nowhere. During those years in the countryside, he'd often joked that if there were some kind of peasant uprising somewhere in the country, he would definitely join it. Like one of the old communists, he'd ride into town and become a leading cadre wallowing in privileges.

Secretly, Wu Zhongyi regretted that he'd missed the Red Army's Long March in the 1930s and the Anti-Japanese War in the 1940s. He was even too young when the Great Proletarian Cultural Revolution broke out twenty years ago. Unlike that Feng Licai, for instance, thought Wu Zhongyi. Through the wind-and-rain storms of the Cultural Revolution, Feng Licai had transformed himself from an anonymous factory driver into a senior deputy Party Secretary and had moved out of a smelly, cramped dorm into a big five-room apartment in a compound where high ranking cadres were housed.

Wu Zhongyi could almost see the tree-shaded residential compound where Feng Licai lived. The compound consisted of five red-brick buildings of four stories high. They had large, impressive cement balconies, carved and painted light green eaves and sloping, golden-tiled roofs. The five buildings faced a center court where there was a well-tended, long, oblong flower bed as well as a big, circular flower bed with a cement border and a fountain in the center. It wasn't that he hadn't waited long enough, said Wu Zhongyi to himself. Hadn't he been waiting for the last fourteen years for something like another Cultural Revolution to come along?

Dad is wrong, thought Wu Zhongyi. You don't have to be big to make a change for the better. But you do have to act. Wu Zhongyi made up his mind to take action.

Housing has always been a problem in Beijing. This was especially so in a factory as big as the one where Wu Zhongyi worked. The housing allocation system was so bureaucratic and full of loopholes that getting anything from a waiting list could be a life-long endeavor. There were more than fifty truck drivers in Wu Zhongyi's team alone, and there were two other teams of the same size.

Wu Zhongyi started to volunteer to do favors for his various bosses. As a truck driver, he was able to help their families, relatives and friends move house whenever needed and to transport goods for them from far away suburban districts or counties. He did all these things inconspicuously, almost as if he were looking east when he was really going west.

Before long, he was favorably recommended and transferred from the truck team to the chauffeur team. Wu Zhongyi became busier than ever. The factory's light blue, Shanghai car that he was now driving could be seen everywhere, day and night, weekdays and weekends. Gradually, he began to know the temperament and hobbies of the important cadres in the factory. He knew exactly the brand of liquor or cigarette they liked or disliked. He knew other things as well.

He knew, for example, that Feng Licai, senior deputy Party Secretary and Director of Acquisitions of Goods and Materials, liked fishing. Every once in a while, Wu Zhongyi would volunteer to drive him to the quiet side of the old imperial canal near the Purple Bamboo Garden in the Western District of Beijing. He wasn't Feng Licai's personal chauffeur.

Wu Zhongyi also knew that, Wan Dongsheng, Director of Housing Allocation, a married man, had a young mistress who lived in a suburb of Beijing. Wu Zhongyi struck up an acquaintance with him and offered him chauffeur service.

The other drivers on the chauffeur team hated to be on call during holidays, weekends or in the small hours of the night. Wu Zhongyi let everyone on the team know that he'd be willing to help them out. He was prepared to drive anytime, anywhere.

For months, Wu Zhongyi put himself cheerfully at the beck and call of all the drivers and their bosses. He earned the reputation of being a "terrific guy, someone you can always count on." People noted how appropriate his name was -- Zhongyi -- which means "esteems friendship."

Wu Zhongyi's old friends, real friends, who'd spent years with him in the countryside as "rusticated youths" after high school graduation, knew his situation and were anxious to help. One hot summer day, Wu Zhongyi's chance finally came. One of his ex-"rusticated" friends, after years of wheeling and dealing, had gotten himself promoted to a managerial position in an expensive, state-run restaurant inside Beihai Park. That friend informed Zhongyi that he'd been able to wangle a special arrangement for a private room with a table for ten people the following Saturday night at the restaurant. He gave Wu Zhongyi the go-ahead to invite whomever he wanted to the free banquet.

The next day, nine cadres of varying importance in the factory received invitations from Wu Zhongyi to attend the banquet at the well-known

Jade Dragon Pavilion by the lake in famous Beihai Park. "An informal dinner," said Wu Zhongyi. "The summer nights are so hot now, and the restaurant is at least air-conditioned. We can try some of the food at the Jade Dragon Pavilion. Nothing fancy. Just a few dishes. We can see if the food deserves its fame. Let me have the chance to express my gratitude to you."

Beihai Park was an old imperial garden which has survived more than eight centuries and five dynasties. Located on the Jade Isle in the middle of the rippling water of Beihai Lake, the Jade Dragon Pavilion continues to be known for its imperial-court delicacies and royal cuisine. Facing the restaurant, across the lake, are the Five Dragon Pavilions and Hall of Celestial Kings. On the hill behind the restaurant, stands the famous White Dagoba.

Around six thirty, Wu Zhongyi's guests began to straggle in for the six o'clock dinner. First came his current boss of the chauffeur team and his former boss of the truck team. Then came the Directors of the Offices of Human Resources and Workers' Welfare. Next came the Union Boss, the Manager-in-Chief of the factory, the Director of Housing Allocation and the senior deputy Party Secretary. Not until seven o'clock, did the main guest, Li Dashan, the short, corpulent, middle-aged Party Secretary, finally arrive.

"Sorry, I'm late," said Li Dashan. "The car got stuck in traffic." He pulled out a white handkerchief and wiped the sweat from his enormous forehead. Walking the two hundred yards from the East Gate of Beihai Park, where the cars were parked, to the restaurant had evidently been rather a strain for the Party Secretary. With a gasp of relief, he sat down and continued to talk.

"This year's summer's the worst I've ever experienced. It feels like a kiln inside our apartment. That's why people are buying air-conditioners like crazy."

"Talking about air-conditioners," said Feng Licai, senior deputy Party Secretary and Director of Acquisitions of Goods and Materials, "most of our apartment buildings aren't designed for the heavy use of electricity. So, we need to make sure that our building is capable of sustaining an air-conditioner before we buy one."

"Lao Feng's observations are always perceptive and helpful," said Wan Dongsheng, Director of Housing Allocation, who was subordinate to Li Dashan and Feng Licai. He then turned to Wu Zhongyi who was sitting quietly between him and Feng Licai,

"Zhongyi, Secretary Li and everyone else has arrived. Shall we start our dinner?" Wan's tone sounded paternal. Wu Zhongyi appeared suddenly to awaken from a reverie.

"Oh, I'm sorry! How negligent of me. I almost forgot the dinner," said Wu Zhongyi. "I'm very glad you could all come. It's been my wish for a long time to have an opportunity like this to express my thanks to every one of you for your kindness and support. I hope the food will suit you, but please forgive me if it doesn't. I really don't know how to order food."

He paused as the waiters brought out the hors d'oeuvres which consisted of cold cuts such as thinly sliced, spiced tongue, tripe, pigs' ears, ham, beef and lamb as well as jellyfish, pickled cucumbers, salty duck and quail eggs and glistening, black "thousand year" eggs. The waiters then poured out tiny glasses of Mao-tai liquor, the best and most expensive in China.

"Let's have a toast!" said Wu Zhongyi, resuming his role as host. Upon hearing this, Wan Dongsheng stood up quickly and raised his cup to Li Dashan.

"Wait a second, folks. Let's first toast our Secretary Li's health. He's worked hard for our factory and given correct guidance for the personal development of each one of us as individuals!" The guests agreed noisily. They all turned to Li Dashan, raised their cups and emptied them of the pungent liquor. Whenever a glass became empty, the waiters refilled it. Wu Zhongyi helped his guests to the hors d'oeuvres, encouraging them to help themselves and constantly filling emptied plates. As the guests chatted and repeatedly toasted one another, some paused to smoke the expensive Zhonghua and Marlboro cigarettes that were provided on plates around the table. In the midst of the din and smoke, the waiters brought out the first dishes -- tender abalone with quail's breast, crispy prawns, clams in a wine sauce, lobster in the shell and scallops and mushrooms sautéed in a light, gingery sauce. The waiters brought out more bottles of Mao-tai, as well as Qingdao Beer, Chinese red wine and orange soda. The room became noisier and smokier, and Wu Zhongyi continued, silently, to fill empty plates.

Half an hour later, the waiters brought out the second course -- Peking Duck, Mongolian roast lamb, Wuxi Lake crabs and steamed fresh carp from Beihai Lake. Wu Zhongyi was busier than ever, passing around pancakes with scallions and plum sauce, distributing freshly steamed carp, and pouring out liquor for his guests. His boss on the chauffeur team spoke up.

"Zhongyi, don't just serve us. You should eat something yourself."

"Zhongyi," said his former boss on the truck team, "are you inviting us to eat a state banquet? How can we possibly finish all these wonderful dishes and wines?"

"I am glad you like the food. Today's Saturday. We don't work tomorrow, so we can take our time.

Eat slowly. There're only a few more dishes coming that we can enjoy together," said Wu Zhongyi.

"More dishes?" said the Director of Human Resources with genuine surprise. "No, no! We really can't eat any more. We've already had too much." Before he'd even finished his sentence, the waiters brought in two more dishes as the last course - Cantonese suckling piglet and the pièce de résistance, braised Siberian bear paws.

"Hwah!" said the overweight Union boss with his mouth wide open. "I've heard about braised bear paws, but this is a first for me."

"Zhongyi, you should've let us know this a lot earlier, so that we could've saved more space in our stomachs," said the Director of Workers' Welfare, trying to be funny.

"Oh, it's nothing. A small matter," said Wu Zhongyi as he continued to ply his guests with drinks.

By nine o'clock, everyone had finally stopped eating. A waiter then brought out bird's nest soup in an ancient light-blue porcelain pot. While noisily sipping the delicious soup, Li Dashan, the Party

Secretary, turned to Wu Zhongyi.

"Zhongyi," he said, "this is a wonderful dinner. But it's too extravagant." Secretary Li wiped his oily mouth with his napkin. "We all know each other very well. So why should you waste so much on courtesy? A simple dinner at home would've done very well. Right?" Secretary Li looked around at the other guests.

The others grunted and nodded in agreement. Wu Zhongyi knew that his moment had finally come. With a self-deprecating and embarrassed look, he said, "I'm truly happy to have been able to invite you to this dinner. I wish I could've entertained you at my own home as well but, well, I don't have one yet."

"I thought you were married and had a child a long time ago, Zhongyi," said Secretary Li with surprise.

"So did I," said Feng Licai, the deputy Party Secretary.

"You don't mean that you have some bad news to tell us about your marriage, do you, Zhongyi?" asked the Manager-in-Chief of the factory.

"Oh, no! Not at all. What I mean is -- pardon me for telling you -- I haven't been working long enough to qualify for an apartment of my own yet. So, even though I'd very much like to, I'm afraid I won't be able to invite you to taste my wife's humble cooking quite yet."

"You should've told me this a long time ago," said Secretary Li, in a chiding voice. "We can at least find you some temporary place until some better housing is available. I'm sure you can move in right away."

"Zhongyi, this is all your own fault," said Wan Dongsheng, the Director of Housing Allocation, realizing that he might become a target for blame. "I've been thinking all along that you had your own apartment. Why have you waited so long to tell us? As Secretary Li said, you should've let us know a long time ago."

"Lao Wan, what's happened to that new apartment building on Tianningsi Road, then?" asked Feng Licai, the deputy Party Secretary.

"Secretary Feng, it should've been completed by the end of this summer, but because of the

June Fourth riots last year, the whole construction has been delayed a year. But the building will be finished and ready by this time next year."

The discussion was temporarily interrupted when the waiters brought out, on silver trays, the famed imperial court pastries. There were dainty corn cakes, each the size and shape of a thimble, exquisite mung bean pastry and various delicate mooncakes, all done in the ancient tradition as they were served to the emperors and their wives.

"Zhongyi, at least we owe you this much," said Secretary Li. "When the building on Tianningsi Road is done, you can pick whichever apartment you want." He then turned to the Director of Housing Allocation and said, "Lao Wan, make sure this time that Zhongyi gets a three-room apartment. If anyone complains, let him come to me, O.K?"

"Zhongyi," continued Secretary Li, "which floor would you like best? The building's going to be twenty-four stories high. Tell Lao Wan, so he can reserve your apartment for you when it's ready next year."

Wu Zhongyi's mind moved fast. He told Wan

Dongsheng that if possible, he wouldn't mind having an apartment on the sixth floor. He knew that to be allowed to use the elevators in the apartment buildings, residents had to live at least on the sixth floor or higher.

The waiters brought out fresh fruits such as lychees and longyans from Fujian, mangoes and bananas from Hainan Island and sliced honeydew and seedless grapes from Xinjiang. The guests were delighted, and the conversation turned to other subjects which Wu Zhongyi would never remember. All he knew was that after the final desert -- Yin'er soup, a sweet, translucent, highly nutritious soup -- he and his guests had consumed a dinner which was worth more than 8,000 yuan. It was the equivalent of seven years of his total annual salary. Luckily, he didn't have to pay a cent, because his friend was the manager of the restaurant. But then, the promised apartment wasn't exactly a reality yet, either, since the building wouldn't be completed until the following year.

Two weeks after the banquet, Wu Zhongyi brought his wife and daughter to visit his parents again. It'd been quite a few months since their last visit, and Zhongyi's father was a little surprised to see them.

"Well, well. And to what do we owe the honor of this visit? What've you been doing with yourself all these months, Zhongyi? Building yourself a house or something?" he asked.

As usual, they sat themselves around the plastic-covered steel table. Wu Zhongyi's short, plump, dark mother was kneading dough at the table. Wu Zhongyi noticed that his father had taken up his grandfather's habit of using a long-stemmed pipe to smoke. The tobacco he was smoking was so powerful it temporarily covered the strong vinegar odor in the yard.

"Oh no. Nothing like that, Dad," said Yulan, who'd agreed with her husband not to tell her in-laws about the banquet. "Zhongyi's just been too tired, lately, to visit."

"Too tired? What's he been doing? Working himself to death? What for? Has he got anything in return? Hard work's not going to get him anything, not even a place like this. You have to inherit!" He cleared out the ashes from his pipe and put in some new tobacco leaves.

"Zhongyi, listen to me this time. Don't try to change things. It's not worth it. Your great grandpa, your grandpa and I have all tried." The swarthy face of Wu Zhongyi's father was wrapped, like a wonton, in a continuous billow of smoke.

"I know you don't want to listen to me," he said. "I was like that once. Like last year, when those hot-headed students shouted for democracy? I'm not saying they were wrong. Not that I care, of course, if we have a democracy or a dictatorship. It doesn't make any difference to us common folks. Power only changes hands not essence."

Wu Zhongyi's mother couldn't hold her tongue any longer. For all Wu Zhongyi could see, she was kneading smoke into the dough. "Oh, for goodness sake. Your Dad's become a sage. Don't listen to him, Zhongyi. The older he gets, the grouchier he gets. Do whatever you have to, as long as it's O.K. with your conscience."

"Conscience? Conscience won't get you anywhere," said Wu Zhongyi's father, snorting and puffing out a particularly large cloud of smoke. "Look at those students last year. Even Party membership doesn't mean anything today. Where's the Party's conscience? The way this Party's going, it's not going to last very long."

"I don't see how you can say that, Dad," said Wu Zhongyi.

'You don't look. You don't listen, Zhongyi. I'll tell you this much. Those students were squashed to death, all right, but not their brains. It only takes a couple of brains to change dynasties."

Wu Zhongyi came away from his parents' shanty house more worried and upset than ever. His father had reminded him of the student movement. Wu Zhongyi had supported the students in his heart. But, with a wife and child, he'd stayed away from Tiananmen Square the night of the massacre. Now, he found that he had a totally contradictory concern. He started to worry about the future of his apartment that hadn't yet been built. He didn't need change. He needed his bosses to stay in power. He needed a person in power who'd remember that 8,000-yuan banquet. He'd never be able to do better than that.

Wu Zhongyi began to have insomnia in his six-man dormitory room. He began to see his apartment melting away like the smoke from his father's pipe. While his roommates snored, he began to pray, silently and sincerely, to whomever might be listening, that the students would hold off on anymore activities until he'd gotten his apartment. "Please, please. Don't let there be any change," he whispered into the air.

FLIGHT

For four days, Yao Lusheng and two fellow villagers had crisscrossed fields and hills around villages and communes, moving stealthily towards a small southern border town called Chegongmiao in Bao An county, Guangdong province. The town was right on the northern edge of Hau Hoi Wan or Deep Bay. Four miles across the bay was Tsim Bei Tsui, a mudflat fishing settlement in the New Territories under Hong Kong's jurisdiction.

This was Yao Lusheng's second attempt to flee to Hong Kong. A year earlier, in July 1973, he and four young men from the same village had attempted to cross the border by land at a point between Shenzhen, on the China side, and Man Kam To. In preparation, he and his friends had found out in detail, from other friends, the location and size of the militia and patrol troops living or stationed in each village, commune and town between Sha Ping, their home village, and Shenzhen, fifty miles to the south. They'd made their own map. They'd even made their own compasses out of razor blades and brass buttons.

That night in late July, they'd crawled through miles of marshland and rice paddies to get near the border. It was almost eerie how similar that night was to this one. In the silent, oppressive heat, all they could hear was the croaking of frogs in the fields. That night, they'd almost reached the six-foot, barbed wire fence. They could see the sentry posts about fifty meters apart and a watchtower in the distance with powerful searchlights mounted on top. It was after midnight. Just as they'd started to crawl out of a ditch and move towards the barbed wire wall, a pack of snarling police dogs had suddenly rushed out at them from nowhere. Yao Lusheng had heard a snarl close by, but before he could run, a guard dog had sunk its teeth into his right buttock. The sudden, searing pain had shot through and paralyzed him. One villager had been bitten so badly that his left fibula was broken.

Yao Lusheng and his fellow villagers were

rounded up, bound and hauled off to military barracks near Shenzhen, where they were imprisoned for a month before being escorted back to Sha Ping, their home village. They were publicly denounced at a meeting on the threshing grounds in the village. As the leader of the runaways and a bad influence, Yao Lusheng had been put under twenty-four-hour surveillance in a dark hut for a week, after which he did two months of forced labor. He was twenty-two years old.

This time, Yao Lusheng had decided to try crossing by water. During the month he'd spent in Shenzhen's military barracks, he'd learned a lot from other captured runaways. He'd learned that the best and the most dangerous route to Hong Kong was by water and that choosing the right time and the right point of departure was of utmost importance. To avoid the sharks in the bay, summer was the best time. Timing was important, too, to avoid being carried to the sharp-shelled oyster beds on the Hong Kong side and, especially, to avoid being swept out by the tides into open seas. When Yao Lusheng was finally released from his two-month sentence of forced labor that year, summer was already over. Autumn was the season for sharks in the bay.

Yao Lusheng had waited quietly for Summer 1974. He knew it was his last chance to make the crossing, for he'd heard that the Hong Kong government was going to close its borders to refugees from China at the end of that summer. It was now August 2, 1974.

They'd been hiding behind shrubs at the foot of a hill, waiting for night to come. All day, it had been unbearably hot and humid. They'd tried to travel light, carrying only canteens of water and some fried, sweetened flour which, with a little water, could be made into an edible paste. Now, after four days, they were almost at the end of their supplies and everyone was exhausted.

None of this worried Yao Lusheng. What troubled him most, at that moment, was the size of his group. The previous night, they'd run into another group of three, including a girl from a village in a neighboring commune. They, too, were heading for the same stretch of water. Together, they could become an easy target. But it was everyone's last chance, so they'd decided to stick it out together. Yao Lusheng now wondered if they'd made the right decision.

The short, skinny girl worried him a lot. Could she survive the long swim through Deep Bay's treacherous waters? Yao Lusheng wasn't even sure he, himself, could make it, and he was strong and used to hard work. But, the last four days on the road had taken their toll.

Finally, it was dark. The air was still hot and oppressive, as the frogs began to croak. A light wind rose, rustling through the leaves of the shrubs that hid them at the foot of a low ridge of hills. Yao Lusheng smelled the ocean. One more hour, and they'd be by the seashore. Then, if they were lucky enough, they would all be on the other side of the bay by morning.

Yao Lusheng moved forward quickly and quietly in a crouch, through the shrubs and the darkness. He was grateful for the gentle swishing of the wind through the shrubs. But, as he moved, he became aware of sounds on the hilltop. People were walking along the ridge, about fifty feet above them.

He heard his companions pushing forward through the shrubs. It was too late to warn them.

"There's someone down there in the shrubs, Captain!" A man with a nervous voice called out in alarm.

From the hilltop, another man's voice, tense and harsh, shouted, "Stop where you are! Don't move if you want to live!" Yao Lusheng heard the clicks of safety bolts being pulled on rifles.

"Come out with your hands above your heads! Don't try anything smart," shouted the same harsh voice.

Yao Lusheng's heart sank. It had happened. It had happened again. His throat burned, and he began to tremble. His legs refused to move. He tried to think, as powerful flashlights swept across the shrubs covering him.

"Listen here! If you don't come out, we're going to start shooting. At the count of five." The man paused. He began to shout.

"One! ... Two! ... Three! ... Four!"

"Wait a second, Sir!" A girl's voice burst out from the shrubs behind Yao Lusheng. Under the flashlights, the short, skinny girl who'd joined Yao Lusheng's group the previous night, moved sideways, out into a clearing. She turned to face the flashlights. Yao Lusheng noticed how young and frail she looked. With her hair in short pigtails, and with a worn-out, green cloth schoolbag and a canteen slung across her pale blue blouse, she looked like a middle school student out on a picnic. Slowly, the girl walked a few steps towards the lights. Suddenly, with the flashlights trained on her, she knelt down on the ground.

"Elder Brothers, Elder Sisters," she said, "Please, give us this last chance. If we had any other way, we wouldn't be doing this. Please, let us go. Have pity on us." She started to cry. Yao Lusheng was taken aback. Everyone was surprised.

"Captain! What's going on here?" said the nervous, young man near the flashlights. "How many are there? We're not going to kill these people, are we?"

"Shut up! Who said we're going to kill them?"

The girl raised her face to the lights, closed her eyes and began to recite something in Cantonese that sounded vaguely familiar to Yao Lusheng.

"The Lord is my shepherd, I shall not be in want, He makes me lie down in green pastures,

He leads me beside quiet waters, He restores my soul.

He guides me in paths of righteousness for his name's sake. Even though I walk through the valley of the shadow of death. I will fear no evil, for you are with me;

Your rod and your staff, they comfort me..."

"She's cursing us, Captain!" said a rude, male voice on the hill.

"She's a witch. She'll bring bad luck," said another voice.

"Let them go, Captain," said the nervous young man. "We don't need bad luck."

"I'll be damned. This is the weirdest night in my life," said the Captain.

"Please let us go, kindhearted Captain," continued the girl. "The Lord in Heaven will remember all your good deeds tonight."

"Listen here! All of you!" said the Captain. "Leave all your valuables on the spot where the flashlights are."

The girl stood up and quickly removed her bag and canteen, placing them on the ground in the oval of light made by the flashlights.

"Empty your bag out," said the Captain.

The girl turned her bag inside out, and a towel, a comb, some bean cakes and a few Chinese yuan tumbled out. She left her bag on the ground near her belongings. Yao Lusheng came out of hiding and did the same. One by one, they surrendered their trifle of belongings, including some leftover food, a couple of old watches and even some Hong Kong dollars. They kept only their inflatable plastic pillows.

The Captain and two other men came down to the edge of the clearing. Yao Lusheng could tell that they were the People's militia, young fishermen on patrol from the local villages. The men cast a quick glance at the objects on the ground, as the Captain shone his flashlight on Yao Lusheng's group. He looked from the girl to Yao Lusheng and back to the girl.

"Listen here," he said, at last. "Go that way." He pointed off towards their left. "You'll come to a small path. Follow it. It'll take you straight to the beach. That's the quickest way. Now get out of here!"

"Thank you, Elder Brothers, Captain. Thank you and bless you." The girl turned quickly, followed by Yao Lusheng and the others.

Yao Lusheng couldn't believe what had just happened. As they moved quietly and swiftly through the shrubs towards the footpath, he half feared the militiamen on the hill might still open fire. But they didn't, and Yao Lusheng was left to wonder at the young girl in front of him. And at their escape. He racked his brains, trying to recall where he'd heard the poem she'd recited.

"Wenlan, you saved our lives tonight," said one of the young villagers who'd joined Yao Lusheng's group the previous night. He moved past Yao

Lusheng to catch up with the girl.

So, her name was Wenlan, thought Yao Lusheng. Quietly, he walked behind them.

"No, Brother Liang. I just did what Sister Ah Fong told me to do. She said if I could remember those words by heart, I'd be all right," said the girl.

"Well, those words of hers certainly saved us tonight," said Brother Liang.

"They aren't her words. They're from Psalm 23 in the Bible."

All of a sudden, Yao Lusheng remembered. It was years ago, when the Cultural Revolution had just started. He was fifteen then. He'd barely dared to look at the scene. His second uncle was beating his white-haired, grand aunt in front of a crowd in the courtyard of her apartment complex in Canton. His uncle tried to make her renounce her faith and burn her Bible. When she refused, he pushed her down on a pile of crushed glass and forced her to kneel there. The frail old lady was wearing an old, black silk skirt with tiny, bright red, embroidered flowers around the pockets. Yao Lusheng could still see the blood, red like the flowers, flowing from her bare knees onto the glass. And he remembered that she'd repeated words like the ones Wenlan had just recited moments ago.

"Maybe we should remember those words, too," said Brother Liang, interrupting Yao Lusheng's thoughts.

"Maybe they'll help us to get across the Bay," said someone else behind Yao Lusheng.

So, Wenlan taught them the words of the psalm, and Yao

Lusheng, along with everyone in the group, tried to remember them.

The Lord is my shepherd, I shall not be in want, He makes me lie down in green pastures,he leads me beside quiet waters, he restores my soul......

Yao Lusheng felt comfort in the words which took his mind off of the formidable swim ahead of them.

The footpath they were following suddenly disappeared. Over a stretch of sand dunes under a cloud-laden sky, flecked here and there with a star, Yao Lusheng saw the massive, rolling darkness of Deep Bay. He heard the crashing of waves along the shore. Deep Bay had served as the route of escape for so many Chinese. And many had never made it to the other side.

Gazing at its broad expanse, a chill crept up Yao Lusheng's back. He took a deep breath. He remembered that his father had asked him not to go. But they both knew that the alternative was only despair. Now, he wondered if he'd ever see his family and friends again. Even if he did survive, he knew that the chances of a reunion were slim.

Silently, they all got ready. Each had brought an inflatable plastic pillow. After making sure that his own was properly inflated and secured, Yao Lusheng quietly helped and checked the others. It was time to go.

"Remember, you're not alone," said Yao

Lusheng, turning towards his companions. It was the first time he'd opened his mouth in hours. "Stick together and keep your eyes focused on the lights across the bay. Don't push too hard; you'll just get exhausted. And whatever happens, don't panic." Yao Lusheng stopped. It took a few seconds for everyone to realize that he wasn't going to say anything more.

One by one, they stepped into the dark water. No one noticed that Yao Lusheng had slipped off his sandals and left them on the beach. He wanted to swim without the encumbrance. In contrast to the hot and heavy night air, the water had a cool edge to it that seemed almost chilly as they were first swept into the furrowed sea. The salty waves, however, seemed less of a threat in the bay than near the shore. The swimmers struck out towards the lights across the bay, floating with the tide, on their pillows, when they were tired. Brother Liang took the lead, and Yao Lusheng more or less covered the rear.

Half an hour passed. It started to rain.

"What shall we do, Lusheng?" asked Yan San, a fellow villager. He was only a yard ahead. Yan

San was a good swimmer, but Yao Lusheng knew that the boy had only thought of the journey as an adventure, a chance, maybe, to strike it rich in Hong Kong. His family was poor, and he was a quick-witted, self-confident boy. But Yan San hadn't fully considered the dangers of the swim. Now, Yao Lusheng could hear the little tremor of fear in his voice.

"The rain is good for us," said Yao Lusheng. "We'll be less visible to patrol boats."

The drizzle turned into a shower, and the sea began to get rougher. With each surge of the tide, they were carried to the crest like little sampans, sliding down into a furrow only to be lifted again. Yao Lusheng felt a heaviness in his arms, as it became harder and harder to move forward. It was too early to be tired. For some reason, the frail figure of Wenlan came into his mind. He tried to locate her among his companions on the tossing waves. The rain obscured his vision and darkened an already dark night. Then, out of the darkness, nearby and to his left, Yao Lusheng heard the girl's soft voice.

She was reciting Psalm 23 again. Everyone soon joined her. They could hardly see each other, but by reciting the psalm together, they felt a moment of shared comfort and protection. Yao Lusheng admired the girl's quiet strength.

When the shower stopped, the waves seemed to grow calmer. Judging the distance from the lights on both shores, Yao Lusheng figured that they had passed the international boundary, which meant they were on the Hong Kong side of the water and halfway through the journey. But he kept quiet. It wasn't time to celebrate, yet. He'd heard too many stories in the Shenzhen barracks. One of his fellow prisoners had made it halfway across the bay, with a friend, when they were attacked by sharks. Despite a torrential downpour, a patrol helicopter from Hong Kong spotted them and came to the rescue, but just as it pulled him out of the water, he saw his friend being torn apart by the sharks in a sea of red. Because of the rain, the pilot had made a quick landing on the wrong side. Hours later, the pilot was allowed to fly back to Hong Kong, but the runaway was thrown into the detention camp at Shenzhen.

"Help, something bit me!" Yao Lusheng heard Yan San's cry. The whole group stopped swimming. Straining his eyes in the direction of the cry, Yao Lusheng noticed that there was no turbulence in the water. He swam quickly over to Yan San.

"Are you all right, Yan San?"

"Something bit me on my right leg. It hurts badly." Yan San started to cry.

"Don't panic. Hold on to your pillow for a while," said Yao Lusheng.

Yan San cried even harder. Yao Lusheng realized, then, that Yan San had lost his plastic pillow. Yao Lusheng unfastened his own and handed it to the boy.

"Here, hold on to this, Yan San. What happened to your leg?"

"Something floated by, and all of a sudden I felt a shooting pain in my leg," said Yan San, holding firmly to the pillow Yao Lusheng had given him. "I thought it was a shark!"

"You wouldn't be here talking to me if it were.

It was probably just a jellyfish. You'll be O.K." Yao Lusheng was relieved. It wasn't time for the sharks, but you could never tell for sure. Of course, he'd heard that some jellyfish stings could be fatal, but Yan San seemed to be all right. The group once again struck out towards their goal, perhaps floating for longer periods of time, now, in their weariness. Yan San shared the pillow with Yao Lusheng.

As they swam and then bobbed up and down like driftwood, a heavy layer of pre-dawn fog dropped from nowhere, clinging to the surface of the water. The swimmers could no longer see the lights, ahead, on the shore. They began to lose their sense of direction. Yao Lusheng didn't know what to do. Mechanically, he trailed behind the group. They'd made it so far. He couldn't bear to think of the consequences of missing the shore, or by some horrible twist, circling back to China.

WenIan's voice then came through the silky veil. Everyone joined her. For the first time, Yao Lusheng seriously recited the psalm, and prayed that whoever controlled his life would spare him and give him a chance to start a new life. Psalm 23 was no longer something simply poetic and comforting. For Yao Lusheng it seemed to be the language of counsel and direction. He followed the sound of the recitation and swam. And, for the first time, he felt oddly calm and without fear. Gradually, the sky began to lighten, and the fog to curl upwards off the water's surface.

"We've made it! We've made it!" Brother Liang was shouting. Yao Lusheng strained his eyes. He saw Brother Liang standing, waist-high in the water against some dim lights along the shore. Like everyone else, Yao Lusheng put his feet down to touch land. Something sharp cut his bare feet. They'd landed on a stretch of oyster beds. The shore was only a couple of hundred yards away, but they had to cross over the sharp edges of vertically planted oyster shells. Yao Lusheng regretted that he'd discarded his sandals. Now he crept over the oyster beds on his hands and knees, floating while he could until the water was too shallow, and he had to stand up. The salty water worsened the pain of each new cut on his feet.

By the time Yao Lusheng made it to the shore,

his hands, feet and legs were covered with bleeding cuts. Despite the pain, he was happy. They'd made it to this side of the world. It was the beginning of a new life.

A couple of seagulls greeted the newcomers, circling above them and screaming noisily. The swimmers spoke to each other in hushed voices in this new world. After a little rest, Yao Lusheng was helped to his feet by Yan San and Brother Liang. As dawn broke, the six survivors of the sea walked towards a mudflat fishing village nearby. It was August 3, 1974.

INSPECTION

Everything was in its proper place, with all the fixtures attached and the last copper and plastic pipes and fittings for water and drainage connected. Yao Lusheng and Han Jiang had finished all the changes that Barry Huang, the owner of the new house, demanded. The repairs to the garage floor and to the joists in the kitchen were also completed. The entire project, to install the plumbing system for the nine-bedroom house, had taken about five weeks. Like some monstrous animal, the house now had a complex digestive system and was ready for the final inspection. It was late November 1995.

Han Jiang watched Yao Lusheng pump air into the sealed water and bathroom pipes again to make sure they wouldn't leak once they were filled with water for the real inspection. The pointer on the pressure gauge maintained a perfect 65. At eight o'clock, they started to let water into the pipes.

The inspection was set at ten. It would require at least an hour and a half to fill the pipes with water from the basement all the way up to the rooftop. Meanwhile, Yao Lusheng and Han Jiang continued to check pipes and fittings throughout the house.

An hour and a half passed. Han Jiang realized that the pipes were probably already filled with water which, at any moment now, would overflow from the outlets on the rooftop. So far so good, thought Han Jiang. No bursting, no leaking.

The worst thing that could happen during the inspection was for a pipe to be found leaking. Yao Lusheng had told him that leaking pipes were a common occurrence during inspections and were expected only to alert the plumber to areas needing attention. Of course, a leaking pipe would mean a failure to pass the inspection and entail the need for another one. But, in this case, thought Han Jiang, it would also give Barry Huang the chance he'd been looking for to discredit Yao Lusheng's professionalism. He might even fire Yao Lusheng without paying him. He could call in another plumber and, for a few hundred dollars, get the project finished up. The more Han Jiang thought about this possibility, the angrier and more worried he felt.

"Water's flowing from the rooftop!" shouted Menglong at the second-floor stairway landing.

Yao Lusheng quickly turned off the water, while Han Jiang rushed to the stairway with a pail full of sawdust which he dumped around the pipe and on the wet stairs to prevent the overflow from freezing over. He used the empty pail to catch the water that was still dripping down one of the pipes from the overflow. Gradually, the dripping stopped. Yao Lusheng and Han Jiang resumed their checking. Han Jiang looked for any signs of leaking as they both worked from room to room. He could tell that Yao Lusheng was anxious and hadn't slept very well. There were shadows under his eyes and stress lines on his forehead.

At ten o'clock, the inspector, Chuck Nelson, arrived, followed closely by an unsmiling Barry Huang.

"Whew! Pretty cold out, today, isn't it?" said Chuck Nelson, blowing out a breath of frosty air and greeting everyone, including Han Jiang, with a nod. His curly, greying, light brown hair looked uncombed, and he was wearing faded jeans and an olive-green ski jacket.

Yao Lusheng and Han Jiang nodded at him and said, "Good morning."

Barry Huang, in his usual grey ski jacket and trousers, scowled at the sight of Han Jiang who looked away blandly.

"Let's get on with it," said Barry Huang, with an irritated grunt. He was evidently more interested in dealing with the task in front of them than with Han Jiang. "Have you fill up the water in the pipe, Yao?"

"Yes," answered Yao Lusheng.

"So, let's start from the garage, then," said Mr. Nelson, going ahead with his inspection. Han Jiang went upstairs again to check if everything was all right. By the time he came down from the top floor, he saw the inspector, Yao Lusheng and Barry Huang all jammed inside the laundry room on the second floor. As he walked towards the room, he heard Barry Huang's loud voice.

"Mr. Nelson. Tell me. Is this a professional work? Is it?"

"What's the problem, then, Mr. Huang?" asked the inspector.

"Look here! Can't you see? Yao removed my floors to put in those pipes. He did the same thing to my kitchen floor, too. That's a problem, isn't it, Mr. Nelson?" Barry Huang bent over the opening in the floor, pointing and complaining angrily to the inspector who glanced down at the pipes.

Han Jiang felt a slight tug at his sleeve. "There's a leak," whispered Yao Lusheng, tilting his head slightly in the direction outside the laundry room.

Han Jiang turned on his heels and left the room. With a rising sense of panic, he walked along, trying to see what had alerted Yao Lusheng. He could see no water, no leaking. But he caught the sound of dripping somewhere in the center room near the entrance. There, he saw water dripping heavily, down a pipe, from the third floor. He grabbed a paint pail, stuffed rags into it to catch the drip and, to avoid being noticed, ran to take the stairs on the other side of the house.

Han Jiang realized that the dripping had come from the bathroom with the super jacuzzi, next to the master bedroom. When he got to the bathroom, he found about half an inch of water already covering the floor. But which pipe was causing the trouble? There were too many pipes and connections -- copper pipes for cold and hot water for three sinks, the shower stall and the jacuzzi, pipes for the toilet as well as black plastic pipes of various sizes for air and drainage. All the pipes looked wet.

Time was crucial now. Any minute Barry Huang and the inspector could walk out of the laundry room and discover the problem. Suddenly, Han Jiang saw water oozing from a 2" plastic pipe above the position for one of the sinks. He grabbed a handful of rags and tried to tie them around the pipe fitting to stop the water, but it was useless. Water continued to ooze out from under the rags.

Han Jiang's heart was racing. He hit his head. Wishing that he'd ask his friend what he should do in case of such an emergency during the inspection, he ran as fast as he could back to the laundry room.

Barry Huang was still complaining about the floors, when Han Jiang reached the door, out of breath. The room was now filled with cigarette smoke from Barry Huang's cigarette. Han Jiang caught Yao Lusheng's eye. He indicated that his friend should come out for a second. Yao Lusheng understood his meaning, but signaled to him, with a slight movement of his hand, that he couldn't possibly leave the room.

Han Jiang left quickly. He was in too much of a panic even to notice, and be grateful for, Barry Huang's obsession with the problem of the laundry floor. All he could think was that the water was still flowing down from the third floor. And, here he was, with all his education and degrees, unable to do anything to stop it.

"This is obviously a sloppy job!" Han Jiang heard Barry Huang shouting in the laundry room. "It will not be the same when the floor put back in place. It will be uneven. When my washing machines and dryer put here, they will shake. It's obviously damaged, Mr. Nelson. Can't you see? It's damaged beyond repair!"

Suddenly, Han Jiang thought of the outlet of the main drainpipe outside the house, down a 4-foot deep hole. Yao Lusheng had put a temporary valve on the outlet and said that all the water in the entire house would eventually go down to that pipe. In fact, the valve had given way from excessive water pressure when Yao Lusheng had tried to fill the pipes the previous day, and all the water had thundered out from the main drainpipe. Han Jiang grabbed a hammer and a wrench, rushed out through the side door in the garage, and headed for the main drainpipe hole.

The sun had come out, but it was still freezing outside. At the edge of the hole, Han Jiang could see down to a thin layer of ice over the water covering the pipe. He quickly let down the water pump, got the water out, and lay a plank part way down and across the hole. From his position on the plank, he tried to use the wrench to loosen the valve. It wouldn't budge. With his left leg on the plank and his right leg in the hole, Han Jiang used his right arm to swing the hammer against the valve. There was a low roar, and the valve flew off under the powerful pressure of the water that instantly filled and overflowed the 4-foot deep hole. Han Jiang's right trouser leg was soaked to the waist, but he was more concerned that Barry Huang might have heard the roar of the water rushing down to this outlet.

Ignoring the ice hardening on his trousers and the sudden, shooting pain in his right side, Han Jiang ran back into the house. He caught a glimpse of the laundry room. They were still jammed in there! And Barry Huang was still arguing and complaining. Then, Han Jiang thanked God that Barry Huang was so greedy, so determined to get the work done for nothing.

Han Jiang bounded up the stairs to the third floor. The pipe had stopped leaking. He dumped pail after pail of sawdust on the wet floor, pushing most of the wet sawdust off to the corners of the room. He then used some rags to wipe away the signs of water on the pipes. Returning to the center room on the second floor, where he'd first seen the dripping, he went to empty the paint pail he'd left by the pipe. Someone had already emptied it and replaced it with a larger pail and new rags! He took this pail outside and emptied it. Going over to the main drainpipe hole, he removed his plank and then returned to the house to continue his cleanup work. The matter of the replaced pail puzzled him. It was then that he began to realize that, all the time he'd been running about, the Chinese and Vietnamese carpenters, whom he hardly knew by name, seemed to have been unusually noisy with their banging and hammering.

After he'd dumped a last pail of sawdust on the wet spot on the second floor, Han Jiang saw Barry Huang emerge, in a cloud of smoke, from the laundry room. He was followed by Chuck Nelson and Yao Lusheng. Chuck Nelson was trying to clear away Barry Huang's smoke with his hand. Yao Lusheng shot a quick glance at Han Jiang. Even from a distance, Han Jiang saw that Yao Lusheng knew he'd solved the problem of the leaking pipe. Slowly, Han Jiang made his way over towards his friend.

"Look here, Mr. Nelson," said Barry Huang, raising his voice again. They were in the kitchen, and he was pointing at the upturned boards on the floor. "You see? He did the same thing to my kitchen floor. Is this a professional job?" He turned around and narrowed his small eyes at Yao Lusheng who was standing behind him.

Mr. Nelson continued his inspection as if he hadn't heard Barry Huang. He carefully examined the correction of a vertical drainpipe in the kitchen that had been moved at Barry Huang's insistence. Chuck Nelson nodded his head approvingly. Barry Huang puffed fiercely on a new cigarette. He continued to stare down at the floor and muttered something unintelligible.

Half an hour later, the inspection entourage moved up to the third floor. After going through various bedrooms and bathrooms, they arrived at the bathroom where the disaster had occurred. Without even noticing the sawdust on the floor, Barry Huang went straight to the jacuzzi to examine it. Han Jiang hinted to Yao Lusheng where the problem had been.

Chuck Nelson went over to the jacuzzi, and casually knocked on one of the pipe fittings. The pipe was obviously empty. He turned to Yao Lusheng and raised an eyebrow in surprise.

"Where's the water?" he asked.

Barry Huang was immediately alarmed by the question. He tapped the pipe himself, quickly turned around and scrutinized Yao Lusheng's face. "What's going on here, Yao?" he yelled. "Why there's no water inside the pipe?"

"Maybe, the temporary valve on the main drainpipe gave way to the water pressure," said Han Jiang, trying to sound innocent.

"I don't believe it," said Barry Huang. He turned to the inspector, and asked, "Is that possible, Mr. Nelson?"

"It's very possible, Mr. Huang," said Chuck Nelson. "Why don't we just go downstairs and check it out?" They all followed him to the main drainpipe hole outside the garage. The overflow was gone, but the bottom of the hole was still filled with some leftover water from the pipe. Above the water, visible to them all, was the valve-less drainpipe outlet.

"What can possibly make the valve go off the pipe, Mr. Nelson?" asked Barry Huang, suspicion written all over his long, gaunt face.

"Water pressure, Mr. Huang," said Chuck Nelson, looking down at the hole. "For the sake of testing the piping system, all the pipes have to be filled with water all the way up to the roof. That way, you know for sure the pipes are full, and you can catch every leak. But that puts a lot of pressure on the pipes, too, especially on the main drainpipe down here."

Barry Huang looked worried, and unconvinced.

"Now, in any normal situation," continued the inspector, "the pipes in the house would never be completely filled even if you were to use all the bathrooms." Chuck Nelson spoke with quiet assurance.

"But who knows whether they fill the water or not in the first place," asked Barry Huang, turning to scowl at Yao Lusheng and Han Jiang.

"That you can ask Menglong," said Han Jiang. "He's the one who warned us that water was overflowing from the pipe on the roof when we filled the pipes."

Barry Huang automatically looked around for his son, but Menglong hadn't been visible since the inspection began.

"But how will I know the pipes have no problem with no water? I think we need another test, don't you, Mr. Nelson?" Barry Huang cast a suspicious glance at Han Jiang's partly wet trousers.

Chuck Nelson frowned and shook his curly head. "That won't be necessary, Mr. Huang. If there'd been any leaking problems, we wouldn't be here talking. We'd have seen the signs. Your house would've been flooded." Han Jiang dared not look at Yao Lusheng.

When they all entered the kitchen in the old house behind the new one, Chuck Nelson went over to the patio table, took out his pen and an inspection sheet, and signed his name to the document. Yao Lusheng had passed the inspection. The ordeal was over. Without saying a word, Barry Huang turned and left the room.

Yao Lusheng thanked the inspector. When Chuck Nelson had wished them both a good day and left, Yao Lusheng said, in a low, excited voice, "Let's get out of here."

They quietly collected their equipment,

including the air and water pumps, and piled everything into the pickup truck. Han Jiang noticed a little spring in Yao Lusheng's step. He was glad to see it, but neither of them said much, yet. The sun was pouring in onto the front seat of the pickup truck as they climbed in. Yao Lusheng backed the truck out of the driveway, and turned onto the road, leaving the house behind them. The nightmare plumbing project was over for both of them.

DEFECTION

"Lao Huang, you look like you haven't slept well these last few days," said a concerned voice opposite Huang Weiguo.

Huang Weiguo turned away from the train window, and tried hard to smile at the speaker, Lao Tang, the portly, grey-haired deputy head of their delegation for the Ministry of Foreign Trade. Huang Weiguo was the member representing the Henan Bureau of Foreign Trade. Along with eighteen other delegates, they were now speeding towards the China-Hong Kong border at Shenzhen and Lo Wu. It was August 3, 1974.

"To be candid with you, Lao Tang, I've never been away from home except when I was in the army ten years ago, and I wasn't married then." Huang Weiguo's answer must have touched his companion. Lao Tang nodded.

"I understand that. Do you have any kids?"

asked Lao Tang in his heavy Shandong province accent.

"An eight-year-old son and a three-month-old daughter."

"So, you've got a son. You should be happy, Lao Huang, eh?"

"Yes, of course." Huang Weiguo found the conversation irritating. He was glad when a pretty young woman attendant in a clean white jacket interrupted them to pour freshly boiled water into their tea mugs from a large aluminum kettle. Huang Weiguo sank back into the soft, upholstered seat with its crisp, heavy beige cotton cover. The compartment, with its rows of identical upholstered seats occupied by the members of the delegation, its ample leg space between the seats and glass-covered tables and its air-conditioning, was clean and comfortable. The air-conditioning, especially, turned the compartment into a cool, pleasant haven from the stifling heat of August. All the buildings in Hong Kong would be air-conditioned, thought

Huang Weiguo.

Lao Tang lit a cigarette and helped himself to a noisy slurp of tea. On the table between them, was a porcelain ashtray containing seven cigarette butts, three of which belonged to Huang Weiguo who turned to look out the train window again. Rice paddies, banyan trees and bamboo-covered hills rolled past, but Huang Weiguo didn't really notice. Lao Tang's mentioning of his son had disquieted him. He thought of the conversation between his wife and his son the night before he was to leave home.

Huang Weiguo had gone to bed early that night. He lay on a bamboo mat, sweating in the still heat of a summer night in Zhengzhou, the capital of Henan province. Not even a stray breeze came through the screen windows. Huang Weiguo had been living in this three-room apartment since he moved from Xinyang county to Zhengzhou seven years ago.

"Is it true that Dad is going abroad tomorrow?" He heard the high-pitched, demanding voice of his son in the family room.

"Quiet, Menglong. Your Dad needs to rest,"

said Liu Cuifen, his wife.

"He's promised to buy me a radio. You don't think he'll forget, do you, Mom?"

"No, he won't. He never does. Now be a good boy and go to your own room."

Huang Weiguo hadn't had time to pay much attention to his son's growth. Only in the past two weeks, had he noticed that Menglong was growing into someone vaguely familiar. Tall and skinny, but rather pale, eight-year-old Menglong reminded Huang Weiguo of himself when he was the same age. That was twenty-six years ago, when the People's Liberation Army had first entered his home village in Xinyang county.

Huang Weiguo still remembered the day. He'd been collecting dung along the one, dirt road that led into his village. The summer sun was scorching, but his tall, skinny, naked body was already so dark and tough that it no longer blistered. From his calloused shoulder, he'd slipped off the wicker basket to collect a large, glistening patty of cow dung when he saw, in the distance, a group of soldiers marching towards the village. Years of war had taught Huang

Weiguo to flee at the sight of soldiers. He abandoned his shoulder basket and started to run, but a familiar voice called out to him to stop. He turned around, and saw his third uncle, Huang Yicheng, among the raggedly dressed soldiers.

"Defu, you little fool. Don't you recognize your uncle? Look at these big brothers and uncles. We've come to beat up the landlords! We've come to get Huang Wanshan!"

Huang Weiguo was called Huang Defu, then. Defu was the name his grandfather had given him, and meant "gets-rich," because the family was so poor. Years later, during the Cultural Revolution, he'd changed his name to "Weiguo," meaning "for-the-country." Eight-year-old Huang Defu wasn't sure he'd understood what his uncle had said. All he knew was that he'd started shivering uncontrollably under the hot sun. He stared at soldiers whose clothes barely covered themselves.

"Don't just stand there looking stupid, Defu. Go and tell the folks in the village that our troops have come. Our village is liberated!"

Liberation changed Huang Defu's life. During

the Land Reform Movement in 1949, the village landlords were dragged out and denounced by the villagers. Huang Wanshan, a landlord who had blood on his hands from having had two villagers murdered, was summarily executed on his own threshing ground. It was with a thrill of joy, and fear, that little Huang Defu watched a soldier put a bullet through Huang Wanshan's bald head. With his death, Huang Defu's family was suddenly released from generations of tenant bondage. In the redistribution of properties, Huang Defu's family got a three-room house, an acre of land and a donkey along with some farming and cooking utensils. What Huang Defu had really hoped for was Huang Wanshan's splendid house, but that was turned into the village headquarters.

A year after the Liberation, Huang Defu started his first year in school and then moved on to the local high school. In 1958, at the age of eighteen, he graduated from high school and joined the People's Liberation Army. After four years of service, he was demobilized and returned to Xinyang. He got work in the Xinyang county co-op as a clerk, married and had a son whom he named Menglong, meaning "dreams-to-be-a-dragon." Huang Defu had made only a sergeant in the army. He now had dragon dreams for his son.

"Comrade passengers, the train will soon be reaching the border at Luo Hu. Please get your travel bags and luggage ready. After going through customs and immigration, you'll board another train to Kowloon. Have an enjoyable trip." Over the loudspeaker, a pleasant woman's voice interrupted Huang Weiguo's thoughts.

The smoke-filled compartment was immediately filled with commotion. Minutes later, Huang Weiguo followed the other foreign trade delegates off the train. In the heat, they walked across the wooden bridge to the Lo Wu-Hong Kong side. They were politely ushered into an air-conditioned guest room and submitted their passports collectively to a Hong Kong immigration officer. When his passport was returned to him, Huang Weiguo noticed the stamped date: August 3, 1974.

After the delegates got on the train to Kowloon,

Huang Weiguo found himself again sitting opposite Lao Tang.

"So far so good," said Lao Tang, relieved when he'd counted heads and made sure that everyone was seated in their assigned seats. The train began to move. Lao Tang lit another cigarette.

Huang Weiguo turned, once again, to look out the window. The scenery hadn't changed much. There were still fields and paddies on either side of the tracks which seemed to hug a river on its west side.

"Lao Huang," said Lao Tang, picking up the conversation again. "You're from Zhengzhou. I used to know a comrade from Xinyang county. His name was Huang Yicheng. He helped our troops liberate the Xinyang region. He was a good person. But I lost contact with him after the war. I often wonder what has happened to him, and where he is now. You haven't, by any chance, heard of this person, have you?"

Huang Weiguo's heart pumped fast. Of course, he knew his third uncle. For a second, he could scarcely breathe, and his tongue seemed to stick to his palate. He shook his head.

"Oh no," said Huang Weiguo. "I don't recall anyone by that name. I was only a kid during the War of Liberation." Lao Tang worked in the Ministry of Foreign Trade in Beijing. He couldn't possibly know about Huang Yicheng's relationship to him, thought Huang Weiguo. He got up quickly from his seat and excused himself to go to the washroom.

Behind the locked door, Huang Weiguo scrutinized his face in the mirror. Had he betrayed himself to Lao Tang? The deputy head had looked so inquisitively at him from behind the clouds of cigarette smoke. Recently, Huang Weiguo had noticed that his hair was starting to turn grey, yet he was only thirty-three years old. In the mirror, a gaunt, brown face looked back at him. He remembered that he used to be quite good looking when he was in the army. He'd been teased about his small eyes, but he was tall, and the uniform had given him presence. He used to run around the track field and do military drills every morning before the barracks. He remembered standing in a crisp, new green cotton uniform in front of the Communist Party flag with its gold hammer and sickle on a red background. He was swearing allegiance, with raised fist before the flag, in the solemn ceremony inducting him as a new Party member. It seemed such a long time ago.

He'd worn that same uniform, faded and without military insignia, as a twenty-six-year-old army veteran, when he'd stood on the platform behind a black microphone mounted on a wooden podium. The faces of hundreds of people were turned towards him. All of Xinyang county seemed to have crowded into the county marketplace that day. And, at the right-hand corner of the platform, had stood his fifty-year old third uncle, Huang Yicheng, with head bent and hands tied behind his back.

Huang Weiguo could almost hear himself shout those fateful words again. "Comrades! Today, I change my name from Huang 'Gets-Rich' to Huang 'For-the-Country.' Today, I draw a clear line between myself and that man. Huang Yicheng is no longer my uncle. I've found out that he was a traitor! All these years, he's been a hidden enemy inside our Party!"

Huang Weiguo didn't look at his uncle when he said those words. After the War of Liberation, his uncle had held the position of Party head of the Xinyang county co-op store. It was through his uncle's influence that he'd gotten the job as a clerk at the co-op after his demobilization. Otherwise, he would have had to return to his village and work on the land.

Huang Weiguo winced, and turned away from the mirror to stare at a corner of the bathroom wall over the toilet. With a strange clarity, that bright, frosty winter day in the county marketplace came back to him - the tense, curious faces of the crowd as they waited to hear him speak about his well-known uncle, the pounding of his heart, the sweat soaking his padded clothes under the uniform and, especially, the bright red blood dribbling slowly down the wire around his uncle's neck and onto the wooden placard. The placard, identifying his uncle as a traitor, was too heavy for the wire from which it was suspended. The wire cut into the old man's neck.

But the placard and the wire weren't his idea, Huang Weiguo told himself. He just hadn't stopped the others from putting them around his uncle's neck. Still, he'd ordered the thing removed right after the denunciation meeting and before his uncle was hauled off to the county prison.

There was just no other way, thought Huang Weiguo. No other way to get out of that hole of a county co-op. The job his uncle had got him provided such a meager income that, together with his wife's salary, they could only bring in 70 yuan a month. His uncle had been able to get him a one room apartment through the co-op, which meant that two-month old Menglong had to sleep with his parents. But the system, being the way it was, he'd never have been able to do any better.

The trouble was, without any new wars, Huang Weiguo hadn't been able to get himself promoted higher than a sergeant before being demobilized. So, he'd had to depend on his uncle's help even to get the co-op job in the county, away from the weary, unpromising life back in his village.

It wasn't that he was ungrateful, thought Huang Weiguo to himself. But a man had to look out for his own family, too. Besides, who was to say that his uncle hadn't betrayed the Party during the War? And if his uncle hadn't liked to brag so much, none of this could've happened. As it was, if he hadn't turned his uncle in, someone else might have.

Huang Weiguo's uncle had been particularly proud of being a former member of the local underground Communist Party during the civil war. In a moment of indiscretion, he'd told his nephew about the suffering and torture he'd undergone for the Party when he was arrested by the Guomindang, the former government, secret agents. He'd almost died. Others in the same local Party cell had died or been killed, but he'd survived and been released. Huang Weiguo guessed that his uncle had survived because he really didn't know anything, but the matter could certainly be regarded as highly suspicious.

When the Cultural Revolution started, Huang Weiguo was fearful and wary. Even though Mao Zedong seemed to be behind the attack against the

Party establishment, he bore in mind the lessons of the Anti-Rightist Movement in 1957, when cadres and intellectuals from the big cities, including the city of Zhengzhou, had been banished to the villages to do forced labor because they'd criticized the Party.

But this time it was different. Huang Weiguo noticed that, following the pattern of the student Red Guard organizations, people in Beijing, Shanghai and other major cities across the country were organizing themselves into many rebel groups. Along with the Red Guards, the rebels started to attack local Party leaders, and some even dared to target major figures in the Central Committee.

Xinyang was a small county. After years of political movements, followed by the three-year, nationwide famine that ended in 1963, people had lost interest in anything but food. Thus, in response to Mao's call to criticize the Party leadership at all levels, the county co-op had only been able to muster a few mild complaints against Huang Weiguo's uncle, written on three, anonymous, big character posters which were pasted to the co-op walls. But Huang Weiguo noticed them, seized his opportunity, and moved with sudden and stunning force against his uncle by revealing that his uncle was the only one in the local underground Party cell who'd survived arrest by the enemy. Innuendo was sufficient to convict.

Huang Weiguo's action against his uncle ignited the local rebel movement. Overnight, he became the well-known rebel of Xinyang county, the defender of Mao Zedong's revolutionary line against a hidden enemy. People flocked to his side, so he organized them into the Regiment of Revolutionary Rebels with himself as their leader. Huang Weiguo reminded his followers that Mao Zedong had said, "To make revolution is justified, and to rebel is right." He told them that they'd done well to choose him as their leader, because he was from among the poorest of poor families, the most trustworthy and glorious category, and because he was a Party member, and had been a revolutionary soldier. That meant, he said, that he was revolutionary by nature and, together, they would clean the Party of revisionists, capitalist roaders, hidden traitors and all those who weren't carrying out Mao Zedong's revolutionary line.

Huang Weiguo soon targeted the county officials. One by one, the rebels brought down the chief of the Bureau of Commerce, the directors of various county offices and finally the chief executive and Party boss of Xinyang County. The rebels gathered evidence and put together files on the personal lives and dealings of these men, dragged them before the public and accused them of anything from a corrupt lifestyle to suppressing the revolutionary masses and carrying out Soviet revisionist or capitalistic policies. No defense was allowed, and Huang Weiguo discovered the pleasure of absolute power.

From the county officials, Huang Weiguo, in his old, green army uniform, the symbol of his revolutionary status, moved on to attack the leaders of the Prefectural Party Committee which governed half a dozen counties like Xinyang. He felt as if a dam had suddenly broken, and his abilities and powers could, at last, flow freely. However, just as his influence reached the edge of the provincial capital, Chairman Mao called for a nationwide cessation of hostilities among the rebels and urged them to unite themselves into one force under a revolutionary committee. The revolutionary committees took over legislative and executive work at all levels. So, at the age of twenty-seven, Huang Weiguo, as one of the powerful prefectural rebel leaders, was selected into the hastily organized Revolutionary Committee of Henan Province. He was now an official at the provincial level.

Someone knocked on the washroom door. Huang Weiguo shot another quick glance at himself in the mirror before unlocking the door. Lao Tang's smiling face confronted him. Huang Weiguo mumbled a few words of apology and let his companion in. Returning to his seat, Huang Weiguo tried to calm himself down by lighting a cigarette and closing his eyes to enjoy the flavor of the tobacco. His position had given him access to good cigarettes. Nevertheless, Huang Weiguo couldn't help picking up his original line of thought.

For five years he'd remained in the same position as a member of the powerful provincial revolutionary committee. From an anonymous county co-op clerk to a provincial official, Huang Weiguo had made a quantum leap. His family had moved from their single-room apartment in Xinyang to a three-room apartment in Zhengzhou, the capital of Henan province. His salary had doubled, and he'd been able to find his wife a better job in the city.

But Huang Weiguo was losing his taste for politics. He'd quickly lost his zest for the banquets and chauffeured cars that came with his position as well as for the gifts from people in need of favors. He had his uncle released from Xinyang County prison at the end of a year, just after he himself had moved to the provincial capital. His uncle, he knew, had then gone back to the co-op where the old man could only be taken on as a clerk because the accusation against him, while never substantiated, had never been cleared, either. With that, Huang Weiguo put his uncle out of his mind.

Nothing, however, could relieve Huang Weiguo's boredom after no more than a year on the revolutionary committee. He realized that not even a cataclysmic event like another Cultural Revolution could catapult him into the enchanted circle of the real wielders of national power. He might, at the very most, work his way into the Central Committee as an obscure voting member, but the rewards, he'd begun to think, might not be worth the effort. Politics didn't offer much more potential and, somehow, was no longer quite satisfying.

Huang Weiguo's attention began to shift elsewhere. With the admission of the People's Republic of China into the United Nations in late 1971 and the normalization of relations with the United States and other western countries the following year, many provinces, including Henan, started to establish their own foreign trade bureaus and make plans for future development in the import and export trade.

Huang Weiguo, again, saw an opportunity, and made himself a deputy head of the newly established Henan Bureau of Foreign Trade. A year and a half later, he became one of the trusted Communist officials selected to represent Henan in a national trade delegation sponsored by the Ministry of Foreign Trade. The moment he knew he was going abroad, Huang Weiguo made up his mind to leave his country for good. From the snippets of information in the internal Party newspaper and documents, he felt there had to be opportunities "out there" that his own country could never offer, opportunities that would allow his powers to flow freely again.

The train stopped at Kowloon Railway Station around noon. In the midst of the bustle and commotion, Huang Weiguo slipped away from his otherwise watchful fellow delegates and disappeared into the crowd. Minutes later, he walked into the local police station.

When Huang Weiguo stepped outside the air-conditioned, Royal Hong Kong Police Station in downtown Tsim Sha Tsui, Kowloon, his new name was Barry Huang. It was four o'clock in the afternoon, and the steamy August air hit him full in the face. Canton Road was congested with cars and buses. Moving northwards with the flow of pedestrians, Barry Huang soon found himself in Kowloon Park. He stopped in front of a lotus pond and sat down on an empty bench under a big Chinese parasol tree. On the other side of the pond, some boys in shorts were playing noisily. Barry Huang watched them from the bench. He noticed, in particular, a tall and skinny boy. The way he ran, scratched his head and moved reminded Barry Huang of his own son. He wondered what Menglong would think of him once the news of his defection had reached home.

BOOMERANG

After his defection, Barry Huang stayed in Hong Kong for three years. During those years, he worked at many jobs, washing dishes, cleaning tables, delivering newspapers and food and, finally, housekeeping and gardening for rich people. Some of his employers were kind and generous; many more tried to get as much done for as little as possible. Whatever the case, he understood, perfectly, that he was nothing but a hired hand. However, Barry Huang was smart. He was always diligent, pleasant, patient and helpful. Anything worth having, he told himself, required hard work and an eye for opportunities. He was sure that one day he would make it. He would be rich and powerful, too. And he would build himself a home that would put all the snobs to shame. Moreover, he would build that home in America. Everyone in Hong Kong wanted to go to America.

Barry Huang tried to get the help of refugee agencies, with no luck. His real break came when the Ng's, a well-off young couple living in a spacious condo in Happy Valley, needed a caretaker for a year. The couple was going to America to try to establish themselves there. They had two boys, one five years old and one eight years old. The woman's widowed mother promised to take care of the children in Hong Kong, but they wanted a responsible, male caretaker to oversee the whole household. Barry Huang had earned himself excellent references and was hired.

Barry Huang stayed with the family a short time before the couple's departure, which happened to enable him to appraise the situation and decide on a course of action. He was well aware that he'd found an unusually harmonious family, one that would value honesty and kindness. Barry Huang received a decent salary, and performed his duties almost impeccably, keeping the young couple regularly informed of the state of the household. He did pocket some of the money given to him for household expenses, but he didn't do it frequently, and the amounts were scarcely noticeable. The money merely allowed him to buy small personal effects without spending his salary. He ran things so smoothly and was so well-liked by the children and their grandmother that they were full of his praises.

Eventually, Barry Huang expressed an innocent wish that he, too, could see America sometime. The young couple knew that, as a refugee from the horrors of Mainland China, Barry Huang had only to find a sponsor to be able to emigrate to the States. Before they returned to Hong Kong, they found him a wealthy sponsor.

In the summer of 1977, Barry Huang arrived in Seattle. He liked everything he saw in and around the city, its waterfront markets, the colorful university district and bustling downtown, and the houses around Puget Sound and Lake Washington. He felt that this was the place for him. He had a small bundle of savings from his caretaker job which he deposited in a bank, and soon found himself a job washing dishes in a Chinese restaurant in downtown Seattle. He worked hard and attended special English classes offered by refugee agencies.

He also listened carefully to what fellow workers said about the city, good and bad. Slowly, he began to pay special attention to trends in the city's real estate business, learning the locations of good and bad properties as well as the general trajectory of their prices.

From his meticulous information gathering, Barry Huang discovered that property prices in the Rainier Valley were plunging because of the increasing presence of drugs and violence as well as a growing gay and transient community. Property owners began to flee in panic, their properties going for ridiculously low prices. Barry Huang decided, then, to make his first deal. He had, by that time, put away enough money to buy a three-bedroom house in the Rainier Valley.

"Barry, are you crazy or what?" asked Victor Wong, a close colleague in the restaurant where Barry Huang had climbed from dishwasher to waiter. "The big noses are all running away from the place. The houses there are no good."

"That's exactly what I'm looking for," said Barry Huang. It was approaching dinner time, but the restaurant wasn't very busy yet. Barry Huang's long face shone in the lights and his small eyes glistened, as he and Victor scanned the few occupied tables. "Maybe the rich guys don't want to live there, but there are people who do -- and badly."

"But you could get mugged or killed in that place, Barry," said Victor, looking puzzled. Barry Huang enjoyed his colleague's bafflement.

"Who said I'm going to live there, Dummy? I've already rented it out. All three bedrooms."

"Rented it out? To whom? What kind of people?" Victor Wong, with his thick, shiny black hair slicked back, stared round-eyed at Barry Huang. The two men had emigrated from Hong Kong about the same time, but Victor was a little younger. As a former native of Hong Kong, fluent in Cantonese, he'd been a waiter at the restaurant for longer than Barry Huang.

"I don't really care, as long as they pay me rent."

"But what if they use your house for drugs?"

"That's their problem, isn't it, Victor? Say they get caught and put into prison. It has nothing to do with me. I can continue to rent it out to the next person, can't I?"

Barry Huang meant what he said. Within two years, he'd collected enough rent to buy another house in the same area. He knew enough about the psychology of the property owners in the area to force a real bargain. Among the owners, Barry Huang was acquiring the reputation of a vampire. By the mid-1980s, he'd bought many properties in the area, including three thirty-unit and two forty-unit apartment buildings as well as a fifty-room motel.

Barry Huang knew the desperate straits of his low-income and welfare clientele, many of whom were new, even illegal, immigrants and uneducated refugees. His rent rates were comparable to those in better parts of the city, but he dropped the lease requirement and lowered the deposit fee. People rushed to put their names on his waiting list. Barry Huang stopped working as a waiter.

Barry Huang's young, Mandarin-speaking real estate agent, Eric Lee, marveled at his client's pursuit of properties in such a dubious area and his evident ability to manage them.

"You must be really smart in your choice of managers," said Eric Lee, in Chinese, one day when Barry Huang stopped by his office to look into other possible prospects. "Sometimes it must be very hard to get rent from your tenants."

"I don't need managers, Eric," said Barry Huang. "I'll be candid with you. Hiring a manager costs money, and he might not be any good. I manage everything myself. Americans don't know anything about management. That's why they can't make any money. The secret lies in management. I don't hire anyone, so I save money. If someone doesn't pay his rent . . .." Barry Huang leaned back into the office chair and stretched out his long legs. There were two other agents in the small, downtown office.

"Well," continued Barry Huang, glancing around and speaking loudly. He looked pleased with himself. "I used to do what the Americans do. I hired lawyers, and that cost money. Too much money! Now, I just file a complaint in court myself. A sheet of paper. Costs me a couple of bucks. If the tenant doesn't pay up on time, the police come in and evict him. I don't have to raise my voice or lift a finger. That's why I go to the court every week, just to hand in complaints. That's the beauty of America. Everything works according to the law."

"But how can you manage so many properties without hiring people, Barry?" Eric Lee was always amazed at how quickly Barry Huang could turn a rundown piece of property into a profit-making venture.

"How? Other people use money to run their business. I use my brains and my own management procedures."

Barry Huang had an office inside one of his apartment buildings, but no one could ever find him there. He had a business phone number, too. But again, no one could reach him. Instead, during business hours, tenants or prospective tenants would find an attractive Chinese lady, in her mid-thirties, sitting behind a desk, answering calls and collecting deposits and rents. Tenants with complaints heard the same answer whether they came to the office in person or called over the phone. The response was always "I'm sorry, the manager is not in the office at the moment. Can I take a message?" The answering machine relayed almost the same response.

The Chinese lady always wrote down any message she was given, though her spoken English was only passable and her writing not very good. Tenants often wondered if she'd understood the message or could convey it properly but, in fact, it really didn't matter. The clogged drains, leaking faucets or roofs, flooded floors, moldy walls, exposed electrical wires and cockroaches remained just as they were. As far as Barry Huang was concerned, the condition of the individual apartments and rooms was the tenants' problem. "I never invited them to live here," he said. "If they don't like it, they can get out!" Almost the only repairs he ever did were those ordered by the county court, which were few and far between.

The Chinese lady was Barry Huang's new acquisition. Her name was Rosa. They'd met at a party thrown by Eric Lee. Rosa was from Shanghai and had a degree in physics from Chengdu University. She'd been sent by China as a scholar to study for a year at the University of Washington. Rosa wanted very much to stay in the States, and Barry Huang was looking for a new wife who would be a low-cost, low-maintenance asset in the home and at the office. Rosa was lady-like, smart and efficient. And she liked, and had a knack for, making money. Eric Lee and Victor Wong attended the simple, September wedding, and Barry Huang took Rosa to the Oregon coast for their honeymoon.

The couple worked well as a team. Barry Huang did the scouting, negotiating, bargaining and purchasing, and took care of the legal and financial side of the business. Rosa took care of the office. With his increasing acquisitions, however, Barry Huang began to feel some pressure. He really needed someone to look into repairs on his properties. Rosa, too, needed someone to help her answer the phone and take messages. Barry Huang wanted her to help with the bookkeeping and to deal with more difficult problems including particularly cantankerous clients.

One day, Barry Huang suddenly thought of his son and daughter, Menglong and Mengxia, back in

China. It was 1986. Menglong would be twenty and Mengxia twelve. In the past, he had, on occasion, wondered what might've happened to them. But he'd never had the time or been in the position to give the matter serious thought. Now, he began to think that he'd like to see them and give them a chance of life in America. It might make good business sense, too. Menglong could be put to work almost immediately to take care of repairs on the properties. Mengxia was at an age to learn English quickly. She could help Rosa with household chores at first and, in a year or two, she'd be able to help out in the office. That way, thought Barry Huang, he wouldn't have to hire anyone. It would be entirely a family business, and with the money saved, he could continue to expand his investments. Of course, Menglong would inherit everything in time, and would carry on the success of the family name.

"I need time," said Barry Huang to himself, "to start thinking about building my house. The Barry Huang Residence. It's going to be magnificent." Barry Huang imagined huge rooms, imposing stairways, a pool, jacuzzies, saunas, gold faucets, plush rugs and marble floors. "No. No marble floors. Too expensive." Barry Huang substituted polished hardwood floors and plush carpets and promised to find himself the best bargains in good materials. "I'll have a party when it's finished. I'll invite everyone I know. I'll hire a photographer and send photos back to people in Hong Kong and China! Maybe, I'll send the Ng's some photos. I wonder where they are. Anyway, I'll show the whole world that I, the peasant boy, the poor refugee from Mainland China, I, Barry Huang, no -- Huang "Gets-Rich" -- have made it in America!"

"Barry? What's the matter?" Rosa's sleepy voice came from the pillow next to his. The room was pitch dark. Barry Huang opened his eyes. He was sweating from the excitement of his whirling thoughts. At that moment, he made up his mind to sponsor his son and daughter to emigrate to America.

Barry Huang had never mentioned his previous marriage and children to Rosa. Once he told her, they had a big fight. Rosa felt both hurt and threatened. She didn't want the children to come.

She wept and wailed. Rosa was normally so cool-headed that Barry Huang was a little taken aback. He thought, however, that he knew how to calm her down.

"Stop crying, Rosa," said Barry Huang. "You'll be O.K. We make plenty of money between us. We'll make even more with the children here to help out. I'm not going to just give everything away to them. I've worked hard to get where I am. They're going to have to work hard, too. You know it would be good to have them here. We wouldn't have to hire anyone, and that would save us a lot of money."

"But after all, they're your children, your own flesh and blood, Barry," said Rosa, wiping her eyes with a soggy tissue as she sat up in the bed. "Before long, you'll feel closer to them than to me. You won't have any love left to give me."

Barry Huang resisted the desire to throttle her. "Don't be a fool, Rosa. You're my wife. We're the family. I want my son and daughter here to help you and me make more money."

"What are you going to do with them, once they're here?" asked Rosa. She sniffled and pulled a clean tissue from the box on the bedside table she'd bought at a yard sale.

"I'll make you a deal, Rosa. Menglong will need to learn something about building and repairing houses. The best way to learn, I think, will be for him to build a house himself. When it's finished, he and Mengxia can live in it, but the house will be in your name. You'll be the owner. I'll send Mengxia to school to learn English. As soon as her English is good enough, she'll be your office secretary. Now, how about that, eh Rosa?"

Rosa nodded reluctantly. It would, of course, be nice to have her own house. But she played with the idea of producing a baby Huang, preferably a male. Her only worry was that, to her husband, the pleasure of having another male heir would be far outweighed by annoyance over the added expenses of raising a child in America.

Barry Huang had lost contact with his family since his defection in 1974. Years later, he'd learned from unexpected sources that, not long after his defection, his wife, Liu Cuifen, had filed for divorce from him. She'd been granted the divorce and had remarried. She'd sent Menglong and Mengxia back to his home village in Xinyang to be cared for by his parents. When his parents died, no one knew for sure where his two children were. After a long search, Barry Huang's agent finally located his son and daughter. In 1988, twenty-two-year-old Huang Menglong and fourteen-year old Mengxia emigrated to America.

As soon as they arrived, Barry Huang put Menglong in charge of the housing construction project and sent Mengxia to school. Menglong learned his trade on the job, though Barry Huang promised to let him take some carpentry classes. Two years later, the son and the daughter moved into a three-bedroom, three-car garage house which Menglong had helped to build. The house was registered under Rosa's name. At seventeen, Mengxia dropped out of school to work for Rosa in the office. Barry Huang's business had never been so good. By 1994, twenty years after his defection, Barry Huang had already acquired more than fifty properties in Seattle, including at least two one-hundred-unit apartment buildings and three dozen smaller ones.

Meanwhile, Barry Huang waited anxiously for his lucky star to shine upon him again. He'd been searching for the ideal site for his dream house ever since Menglong and Mengxia arrived. Through Eric Lee's real estate agency, Barry Huang eventually learned that a Colorado banker who owned a big, old house by Lake Washington was in financial trouble and wanted to sell his property for a quick and substantial amount of ready money. Barry Huang paid out around half million dollars and acquired a piece of property worth double that amount. From that day on, the focus of Barry Huang's attention shifted to his dream house by Lake Washington.

***

Menglong was galled by his father's refusal to lend him anymore money. He knew, of course, that his father was shrewd, and had probably smelled something fishy about the failure of the previous investment scheme in China. But, thought Menglong, the old man had plenty of money, and could afford to lose a little more.

It was cold and grey outside as Menglong

examined the plastic sheeting that he'd ordered erected along the lakefront to stop debris from sliding into the lake. They'd been fined almost $300 by the county for sanitation violations, and Barry Huang had nearly hit the roof. Menglong pulled the zipper of his thick, light brown work jacket all the way up to his chin.

There had to be some way of getting more money out of the old man, he thought. He wasn't going to let his father get away with the way he'd treated Mengxia and himself. Whenever he thought about what had happened to him and his sister, Menglong tasted pure bitterness welling up from somewhere deep down inside himself.

As soon as Menglong and his sister had arrived in Seattle in 1988, they were put to work for what Barry Huang called their "room and board." Even during the few years when Mengxia was sent to school, she worked part-time in the office with her stepmother.

During the day, Menglong worked on a housing project. His father had told him that, after its completion, the house would belong to him and Mengxia. At night, Menglong was frequently called by his father to run errands and do emergency repairs on the various properties. After two years' hard work, Menglong and Mengxia moved into the house Menglong had been working on. They soon learned, however, that the house in fact belonged to Rosa, and that they would have to continue to work for their father and Rosa to pay for room and board.

Every time Menglong asked for money from his father, he would get the same answer. "I provide well for you and your sister. What do you need money for? Now you both have a house, a car and jobs. What else do you want? If you're worried about how you're going to get married, don't worry about it. In America, the bride's family pays for the ceremony. Besides, I'm your father. I'll take care of everything."

Finally, a year ago, and six years after he'd arrived in America, Menglong proposed an investment plan. He'd been thinking about it for some time and had made the suggestion only after he felt fairly sure of his father's confidence in him.

One evening, early last May, after completing

some major repairs on one of the properties, Menglong went to look for his father. The evening was unusually mild, and all the rhododendrons, on the street where his father's house was, were in brilliant bloom. Even, he noticed, the scarlet and mauve ones in front of his father's modest, two-story house in Renton. It was a good sign. He found his father reading the newspaper on the old, green couch in the living room. Though the windows were open, the smells of dinner were still in the air.

Barry Huang looked up warily from the newspaper as Menglong entered the room.

"Dad," said Menglong. "I've finished the repairs at the Cascade Court."

Barry Huang grunted. That was indeed good news, and he was pleased.

Menglong sank into a worn, green velvet covered armchair near his father. "Dad, I want to talk to you about business."

Barry Huang laid aside his paper and squinted at Menglong. A wary look again crossed his long, gaunt face.

"I've just heard from a friend in Hong Kong."

"How do you know anyone in Hong Kong?"

"I was in Shenzhen a couple of years before your agent found me there. And I noticed that the quickest and surest way to make money, to make a lot of money in China, is to invest in real estate. But, well, you know how important connections and influence are in China?"

Barry Huang nodded.

"My friend, Yan San, knows some very important people in Shenzhen. They have a military background and political ties to the Central Committee. And they know where and when to buy land which is going to go up in price."

Barry Huang began to look interested. "So, who is this Yan San? How did you meet him?"

"Yan San swam across Deep Bay in the early 70s. In 1985, he went back to China. He said he was a Hong Kong merchant. I helped him a lot in Zhengzhou when he first came back to scout the market. We even shared a room. The next year, I met Yan San again, in Shenzhen. I was doing some trading there in tobacco and medicinal dates."

"Medicinal dates?"

"A new product of our own home province, Dad," said Menglong, evasively. "Anyway, I was staying at The Golden Phoenix, one of the best hotels in Shenzhen." Seeing his father frown, Menglong added, "At the expense of our company which was run by the Henan provincial bureau of agriculture."

"Why haven't you ever told me this before?" asked Barry Huang, sitting forward on the couch to scrutinize his son. There was something open and frank about the boy. But one had to be careful. With some pleasure, Barry Huang noted, though, that Menglong was well-built and rather good looking. Luckily, the boy was also smart, a quick learner and very handy.

Menglong looked his father in the eye. "I told you I was doing some trading when your agent found me, Dad. But I guess you were too busy to think much about it."

It was true, of course. Barry Huang knew he hadn't paid much attention to what Menglong had said. He'd only been interested in getting his son to learn the construction business. He grunted.

Menglong, too, was sitting forward in his armchair, and looked earnest.

"How well do you know this Yan San?" asked Barry Huang.

'We're very good friends. He took a liking to me and said the kind of business I was doing was too small. What he did was invite some of the big people in Shenzhen to very fancy banquets at the best restaurants. He gave them some pretty large gifts, too. He was originally from the area, so he knew a lot of people. Anyway, he got some important inside information about where and when the price of a piece of land was going to be worth millions. He sold this information to his connections in Hong Kong. They bought the land while it was cheap, and then sold it for ten to twenty times their original investment. Of course, there were more kickbacks for the big guys in Shenzhen, too. Yan San is really rich now. He knows the system inside out, and wherever he invests he strikes gold."

"So, you're still in touch with him, eh?"

Menglong knew that his father was almost hooked. "Of course," he said. From the pocket of his grey, neatly pressed, cotton trousers, Menglong pulled out a folded envelope. "Last week, he wrote to me. He says that he's gotten wind of potential development in the Pudong District in Shanghai. Hong Kong returns to the mainland in 1997, and the government is thinking of shifting its investments from Shenzhen to Shanghai. They want to rebuild the city into one of the world's largest financial centers. Yan San says that he's going to invest big time in the area before anyone else moves in. He offered me a chance to join in, but we have to act quickly. Here's the letter he wrote me. You can see for yourself, Dad."

Barry Huang turned the envelope around in his hands. It was obviously of very good quality and bore the logo "The Hong Kong China Trading and Investment Company" in unostentatious black letters. The address was in downtown Hong Kong. The letter itself was on matching paper, and the office's fax and phone numbers were given. Barry Huang read the letter.

"Let me fax this number, Menglong," said Barry Huang. "I want Mr. Yan to send me some information about his company."

Menglong agreed immediately, which allayed any qualms his father might have had. They faxed the request together from Barry Huang's study. When Barry Huang got the reply, he was satisfied. Menglong said they'd have to be up-front with ready cash. Rosa found out, and was a little alarmed, but Barry Huang told her he wouldn't risk a lot of money. Still, he'd have to invest enough to get a good return. A little over a week later, Menglong was dispatched by his father to China with $200,000 in cash.

Menglong spent three months in China and Hong Kong before returning to Seattle, in August, with bad news. He told his father that his friend's company had just gone bankrupt, and that they'd lost all of the $200,000 investment.

"What kind of fucking friend do you have, Menglong?" shouted Barry Huang. "Didn't you say it was a sure thing?" He paced the living room in his faded, grey polo shirt and khaki shorts. The day had been hot, but the evening sky had clouded over and there was a good breeze.

"But there's a certain risk in all business, Dad. You know that," said Menglong. He was again sitting in the green, velvet-covered armchair, in T-shirt and shorts. "Yan San's most important connection was a high-ranking cadre's son. He was Yan San's most trusted business associate in China, and they made a lot of money together. But who would've thought the government would suddenly decide to crack down on corruption again? Yan San didn't know his connection was involved in huge, shady deals. Yan San put his company on the line, so he had to declare bankruptcy." Menglong knew that his father wasn't fully convinced by his explanation.

In private, Menglong celebrated his success. Apart from what he'd paid out to Yan San and what he'd squandered in Hong Kong and China during his three-month sojourn, he now had $100,000 in his own bank account. Yan San, who was dealing in such items as videotapes and CD-ROMs, had proved to be an invaluable friend. Menglong told his sister not to worry about the future, and that he would take care of her, but he refused to explain anything.

As Menglong walked back to his father's

grand, new house after inspecting the plastic sheeting along the lakefront, he thought, with some pleasure, of how he'd thwarted his father's attempt to force Yao Lusheng to pay more for the damage to the joists in the kitchen. Not that he cared particularly for Yao Lusheng. But his father had said that he, Menglong, was in charge of the project and was paid well for his responsibilities.

To hell with his lies, thought Menglong. He quite enjoyed the look on his father's face when he'd told Yao Lusheng it would take only two and a half days to repair the joists, instead of the ten days to half a month his father had suggested. Had his father been willing to pay him even a fraction of the $366 per day salary, thought Menglong bitterly, he would've backed the old man's lies all the way.

Menglong was only two months old when the Cultural Revolution started. All he could remember was that his father was very busy and didn't spend much time at home. Even then, people were constantly coming to see the family. Menglong was three years old when his family moved from Xinyang to their much bigger apartment in

Zhengzhou city. He wasn't quite sure what his father did, but he enjoyed the attention of everyone who called on him. The residential compound in which Menglong lived belonged to the provincial government and housed only the families of high-ranking provincial cadres. The compound was tree-shaded and pleasant and had a gatekeeper. Menglong was proud to live there and to be greeted by the gatekeeper whenever he went in or out with his mother. By the time he enrolled in school, he enjoyed the envy of his schoolmates. He used to brag about his father's position on the provincial revolutionary committee. On more than a few occasions, when schoolmates, or even teachers, ignored his demands, he threatened them with reprisal from his father. He discovered that, among the teachers, at least, this had some effect. Then, things changed.

One night in August 1974, about a week after his father had left China with the foreign trade delegation, a group of people, some of whom were his father's colleagues suddenly burst into his apartment in the compound. Menglong was eight years old. He never forgot the scene. He remembered the horrified look on his mother's pale face as she was rudely brushed aside by a man he'd always known as Uncle Teng.

Uncle Teng used to visit regularly, bringing him candies and other goodies. Menglong knew that Uncle Teng worked for his father, and that his father had always made fun of the tall, awkward young man, saying how stupid he was. Now, Uncle Teng had brought in this group of unfriendly people, including two policemen, who were going through his family's belongings. He saw Uncle Jiang and Uncle Li ransack his father's desk. Uncle Teng pushed his way into the bedroom where Mengxia, who was only three months old, had just been awakened by the noise and had started to wail. Uncle Teng hauled Mengxia out of the bed and shoved her into her mother's arms.

"You take that baby outside, you hear me?" yelled Uncle Teng. Menglong started to cry, wondering why Uncle Teng was suddenly so unkind.

"What's going on, Lao Teng? Has something

happened? Has Menglong's father done something?" asked his mother in a trembling voice. She held Mengxia tightly in her arms and pressed Menglong to her side.

"What do you think has happened?" asked Uncle Teng, looking down coldly at her. "Don't tell us you don't know!" The two policemen came over to his side.

Menglong's mother began to cry.

"You know, don't you? You planned it together!"

"No! No! Please, Lao Teng. Tell me exactly what has happened. I need to know."

"Your husband is a traitor. He betrayed the trust of our Party and our country. The minute he got off the train in Hong Kong, he defected. That's what's happened!" Lao Teng spat on their floor. "Now stop that bastard son of yours from hollering. We've got work to do."

Menglong's mother, with Mengxia in her arms, dragged the boy into a corner of the living room. She held Menglong so that he couldn't see what was happening. The searchers found nothing special and left. Only then did Menglong see the chaos of scattered papers and overturned and broken objects throughout their rooms.

A month later, Menglong's family was evicted from their apartment. On a bright, warm, sunny September day, his mother took him and Mengxia to the railway station in Zhengzhou. He remembered that the gatekeeper had paid no attention to him as he left, with his mother, to catch the bus to the station. At the station, a tall, grizzled stranger from his father's home county was waiting for them. His mother was crying very hard. She hugged Menglong tightly and told him that the man was his third great-uncle. She then handed Mengxia over to his third great-uncle and, without saying another word, turned around and hurried away from them into the crowd. Confused and frightened, Menglong had tried to run after her, but was held back firmly by the stranger. He kicked and screamed and cursed, but all in vain. He was pulled onto the train which had started to move. That was the last time he saw his mother.

The next five years, Menglong and his sister

lived with their grandparents in his father's home village in Xinyang. His grandparents were poor and ill. They'd had only one son, Menglong's father, and therefore had no one to help earn work points doing farm work. With the arrival of the children to live with them, the last bit of financial help from Menglong's mother dried up. Only later, did Menglong come to understand that his mother had drawn a clean line between herself and the traitor's family, including the children.

Menglong was constantly hungry and prowled the village for food. Many times, he crawled into other villagers' private vegetable plots to eat their half-ripened tomatoes, cucumbers and eggplants. More than once he was caught and beaten.

At age ten, Menglong quit school, and started to work full-time as a cowherd for the production brigade. Every morning he would get up early and lead the herd of half a dozen lean cattle out of the village to graze in the hills while he cut grass for them to eat at night and collected dry, fuel wood for his grandparents.

For three years, Menglong worked as a

cowherd. With his dark, dirty face, rough hands and bare feet and his worn-out straw hat and tattered pants, Menglong could easily pass for a typical village boy. But he had a bitter and angry heart that few village boys would have understood, and Menglong neither wished to join in their games nor was invited.

A little over five years after he and his sister joined their grandparents, his grandfather died. About a month later, his grandmother died. Thirteen-year-old Menglong felt yet again abandoned. He knew that Mengxia felt the loss of their grandmother more than he. She'd been mouth-fed pre-chewed food, like a bird, and washed, cared for and loved by Grandma. When five-year-old Mengxia understood that Grandma wouldn't be around anymore, she howled so terribly that Menglong was frightened. He carried her around, trying to console her, but all he could think of was the disappearing figure of his own mother, in her dark blue trousers and pale blue, short-sleeved blouse, as she hurried away into the crowd at the railway station. He hated her with all his heart.

The children's third great-uncle came to the village and took them to live with him in the apartment complex belonging to the old county co-op which was now part of the city of Xinyang. The old man was kind to the children, but soon, from various remarks by other members of the family, Menglong found out that his father had betrayed his great-uncle during the Cultural Revolution. The more kindness the old man showed him and his sister, the more ashamed, bitter and angry he felt about his father.

Years of cow herding in the village hills, moreover, had left Menglong unable to focus on school. He began to cut classes and associate with people of rather shady background. At the age of fifteen, he ran away and joined other delinquent teenagers in the city. He was in and out of reformatory schools, thereafter, until he began to do a little in the way of trading in local agricultural, textile and woven products, delivering them to different parts of the country. In 1985, in Shenzhen, he met Yan San who was dealing in genuine and fake products of all kinds in both Hong Kong and

China.

When he was finally located by Barry Huang's agent in Shenzhen, Menglong had just begun to make enough money to support himself and even to help out his sister whom he'd encouraged to stay with their great-uncle. He sent her money, in the hopes that his great-uncle's family would be kind to her. The old man was always kind, but the money Menglong sent his sister aroused some jealousy among the other family members. Mengxia was very unhappy. Just as Menglong was considering what to do, he learned that his now rich father was looking for him to bring him and his sister over to the United States. Menglong saw the possibility for revenge.

***

Barry Huang looked at his watch. It was already three o'clock in the afternoon. Three hours had passed. No one had showed up for the twelve o'clock party. The beautiful, hot June day had suddenly turned dark and nasty. First came a strange, fierce wind out of nowhere. It lifted the black and white, checkered plastic tablecloths on all the small patio tables around the lawn, scattering paper plates and Styrofoam cups everywhere. Barry Huang ran from table to table trying to hold down the tablecloths, furious that nobody was helping him. Then, the storm broke with thunder, lightning and rain. The tables were overturned, chairs were crushed, and food lay all over the muddy lawn.

"Where are all the damn people?" shouted Barry Huang. "Can anyone hear me?" Everything was ruined. All the food was spoiled.

Standing on the lawn, in the rain, Barry Huang felt like a soaked chicken. He turned slowly to face the front of his house. It wasn't finished! He'd been too anxious and sent out the invitations too early. No wonder no one had come. Under the dark clouds and drenched in the storm, the house, with its grey cement walls and red roof, looked like some monstrous red-crowned crane. Thunder shook its body. Barry Huang could have sworn that the lightning made it look like it was blinking. Gradually, it seemed to rise. Under its enormous body, Barry Huang saw three skinny legs. The monster hobbled towards him like a giant toddler.

One, two, three...

One, two, three...

One, two, three...

Step by step and by step, it moved nearer, nearer and nearer. Barry Huang was terrified. He couldn't move. He was right under it. He could feel its weight. It was going to sit on him. It got heavier and heavier. He could hardly breathe.

"Help!" he cried.

"Help!"

"Help!"

"Barry! Barry! What's the matter?" Rosa's foggy voice came from the pillow next to his. She nudged him. "Wake up. It's a dream. You're having another dream."

Barry Huang woke up sweating. The room was pitch dark. He looked at the digital clock on the bedside table. It was only three o'clock in the morning. He'd been having bad dreams ever since he started to build this house by Lake Washington. Only recently, the nightmares had grown more bizarre. This one was the worst.

He got up from his bed, put on his worn, grey

terry cloth gown and went into his study. Turning on the study lamp, he sat down in an old swivel chair in front of his desk. The room was small. Pinned to the cork board on the wall in front of him were some color photos of the outside of the house by Lake Washington in various stages of development. The center one had been taken only a few weeks back.

On the desk against the wall behind him, covered by a yellowing plastic sheet to keep off the dust, were his computer, printer and fax machine. The rest of the space was taken up by secondhand grey, green and black metal file cabinets of various sizes. Each cabinet was securely locked. His desktop was empty except for a digital clock, and all the drawers were locked.

Barry Huang unlocked one of the drawers of his desk, pulled out a legal pad and a pen, and started thinking. Three more weeks. The new house would be completely ready. The new, grey rug was now in place. That had cost him a bundle. He frowned.

The whole house had cost him a lot. Luckily, the store had had to sell the rug to him cheaper because he'd found that little difference in shade. It wouldn't be noticeable, really, on the floor. But it was there. Even the store manager had to agree.

If it hadn't been for those damn articles in the newspaper, everything would be perfect. Now, just as he was getting ready to add the last touches to the new house, both Pierce and King counties had threatened him with a thorough investigation of all his properties. He just did not need this kind of trouble, now. The house by Lake Washington required his full attention.

Barry Huang's mind flew back to a fortnight earlier. The rug company had done a shoddy job of laying the rug in one of the small bedrooms. He had to watch their every move. And Menglong had brought over the written warnings from the county offices. In the evening, Menglong had driven over to talk to him. The boy was getting to be quite useful. He'd suggested that rather than let the county investigate and slap them with fines and maybe even closures, he could do at least a quick, superficial improvement of all the properties and deal with all the flagrant violations so that the properties would pass a basic, general inspection.

Menglong had offered to survey all the properties and present his father with an estimate of the cost. Barry Huang, sitting in front of his desk and playing with his pen, felt his stomach tighten. Last week, Menglong had come to him at the new house and told him that with about $500,000, the overhaul could be done in less than two months.

"Five hundred grand!" Barry Huang had shouted.

"Look here, Dad," said Menglong, who'd laid out computer printouts of his estimates for each of the properties. "You have sixty properties, and they're all in pretty bad shape. I can't do all the work myself. We want to do this fast. The counties are after you and you know that. This is my estimate if we make just the minimum repairs. I need to buy all the materials. And we need to hire carpenters and painters. We need to hire movers to help people relocate temporarily. I can handle some of the electrical wiring, but I'll still need some help with so many properties. I can probably get Yao Lusheng to handle the really bad plumbing problems. He's pretty cheap."

When Menglong mentioned the plumber, Barry Huang had inwardly balked, but he knew his son was right. Yao Lusheng was not only cheap; he actually did quite reasonable work. It wasn't the plumber who bothered Barry Huang. It was that assistant. Han Jiang had a brash, self-righteous, powder-keg ferocity about him that had the mark of the Red Guard.

Barry Huang squirmed as he thought, again, of Han Jiang, tall and solid, in his grey sweatshirt and faded khakis, shouting at him, accusing him, judging him. The incident had churned up old, dark memories of his third uncle and the other men he'd brought down. For a moment, Barry Huang felt afraid. It was just as well, he thought, that he'd agreed to let Menglong oversee the renovation project.

Menglong hadn't even noticed his father's reaction. He merely continued to point out that, by investing a relatively small sum, Barry Huang could avoid any fines and ensure that all his properties would remain open and continue to bring in money.

Barry Huang had gone carefully over Menglong's estimates, and suggested some places where he might cut back, but on the whole, the boy seemed to have made a pretty reasonable estimate. And he hadn't charged anything for his own labor. Barry Huang knew that Menglong was capable of handling the project. He liked the idea that his son seemed to view the properties as a family business. He thought that, perhaps, Menglong had realized that one day he'd inherit the business.

Barry Huang's attention returned to the legal pad in front of him. He told himself that Menglong's offer to help out at this crucial time certainly took some of the pressure off of him. He could focus on getting the furniture for the new house. He wanted everything to look its best. Rosa had good taste. The trouble was, he couldn't trust her to get the very best bargains on the furniture. He'd have to go out with her. She could choose the style and color, but if he couldn't get the right price, she'd have to make adjustments. And then he'd have to make sure all the furniture got to the house in good shape and was put in the proper place. He didn't want the movers to scratch his doors and walls.

Three weeks should do it. Then he could have his party. Barry Huang had even ordered an expensive dinner set and glassware. He knew he wanted the China Royal Palace to do the catering. It was the most expensive Chinese restaurant in Seattle and could prepare excellent seafood. He also knew exactly what he wanted to order. He wanted the best, of course. He'd have plenty of everything, including the best-known wines and liquors.

Barry Huang also wanted to hire a professional photographer for the occasion. He wanted to send pictures of the party and the house to people back home in China. He wanted them to see that the poor peasant boy had made it in America.

But whom was he going to invite to the party? To whom would he send the photos? These questions had been baffling him ever since he'd seen the completion of the house as a fast approaching reality.

"How about Eric Lee, your real estate agent?" suggested Rosa, once.

"The son of a bitch has been avoiding me as

if I have some infectious disease ever since those articles appeared in the newspaper!" shouted Barry Huang. "I might as well invite a dog off of the street!"

The articles certainly hadn't done him any good. People with whom he did business on a daily basis, he noticed, had started to give him strange looks or evasive answers whenever he spoke to them. Like that oily, young son of a bitch, Martin Lum. Who was Martin Lum to stick his nose up at him, Barry Huang? Hadn't he just come from Hong Kong and begged for some real estate tips? Now Martin Lum was running a thriving apartment business, too, and had stopped answering Barry Huang's calls.

It was equally irksome that even total strangers, like that pimply-faced, young clerk at the stationers in the nearby plaza, now gaped at him in sudden recognition. Luckily, Rosa did most of their shopping. No one knew her. Barry Huang knew that such incidents of recognition by strangers would blow over, and the newspaper articles would soon be forgotten. But his snooty neighbors wouldn't even say "Good morning." And the damage done to his reputation among business associates would need some smart management.

"At least you can invite Victor Wong, your old restaurant friend." That was Rosa's last suggestion.

"What?! That loser? He's on welfare. He got too old to be a waiter and got laid off. Besides, he's not my friend. He never was. We just happened to work together in the same restaurant." But it was a thought. Barry Huang wasn't sure, though, whether the pleasure of showing off his new house to Victor Wong could make up for the awkwardness of having him around the people he wanted to impress.

"How about some of your old friends from the university, Rosa?" Barry Huang had asked her one afternoon when he'd sat down, yet again, to try to draw up his list of guests.

"Oh, Barry," said Rosa. "You know I lost contact with everyone over the years. Except for Elsie Ren. I'll invite her, of course. But I don't know if she'll have time."

Barry Huang swore, under his breath, in the Henan dialect. Elsie was from Shanghai, like

Rosa. The two women had met at the University of Washington. But Elsie was a sharp-tongued busybody. Barry Huang knew that Rosa poured all her troubles into Elsie's ear. Elsie was always critical of him, always looked sideways at him out of those little piggy eyes of hers. Still, she'd been glad enough to visit with Rosa at their home. Since the newspaper articles, however, Elsie had stopped visiting, and Rosa had taken to spending time at Elsie's home. He had to watch Rosa, and make sure she wasn't neglecting her side of the business.

The telephone rang. Barry Huang glanced at the digital clock on his desk. It was 4:10 in the morning. Rosa had obviously caught the call on the second ring. It was probably a wrong number, he thought. Or, some stupid prank.

"Barry! Barry!" said Rosa, pushing open the door of his study. She'd wrapped her pink and white chenille gown around herself so hastily that one side of her hem was a foot shorter than the other. Her hair was in disarray.

"Menglong's on the phone at Sea-Tac airport!"

Barry Huang whirled around in his chair,

flipped aside the plastic sheet over his fax machine, and picked up the receiver. A loud buzz came over the line.

"Oh! He hung up! I asked him to stay on the line, to talk to you." Rosa began to sniffle.

Barry Huang looked at her, his eyes narrowing as he waited impatiently. His heart began to beat quickly.

"Menglong said he and Mengxia are going back to China! It's a China East flight, and it leaves at 4:15," said Rosa. She looked at the clock, and said, "Oh!" It was 4:13.

China? China? Barry Huang seemed to hear the blood rushing into his ears. He felt a pain in his chest, as he thought of the $500,000 account he'd made available to Menglong. He seemed to hear Rosa calling his name, but everything went black.

Three weeks later, Barry Huang was well enough to drive by himself back to the house by Lake Washington. By then, he knew that, aside from cleaning out the $500,000 account, Menglong and Mengxia had taken only a few clothes and some photo albums with them. They'd left the house built for Rosa in good condition, but Rosa had to get rid of a dozen boxes of their miscellaneous belongings. Apparently, they'd gotten their American passports, too. Menglong and Mengxia had evidently planned their flight for some time.

"I'll find them. I'll catch them! I'll take them to court!" said Barry Huang to himself.

Barry Huang sat, tiredly, at his desk. His properties were still in bad shape, and the county was preparing to investigate. The furniture for the new house hadn't been bought yet. He looked at the photos of the new house on the cork board. The blood seemed to surge to his head, again. Barry Huang reached out, tore the photos down, and flung them around the room.

About the Author

Quan (John) Zhang received his BA in English in China in 1983, his MA in American Literature from the University of Keele in England in 1985 and his Ph.D in American Studies from the University of Maryland at College Park in 1993. He pursued his writing while working at the University of Washington Law Library and continues to write in his retirement. His work in English has appeared in numerous journals including:

"Colonel Ma's Father," the Winter 1996 issue of Folio: A Literary Journal https://1drv.ms/b/s!AlDbHVZtizQh3hGW9r 24FcS0zJEc

"The Balcony," the 13th Anniversary 1996 (Vol.30 Nos. 2- issue of Wisconsin Review
https://1drv.ms/b/s!AlDbHVZtizQh3g7Mcdhtj HjxogJy

"The Birds & Bees in Beijing," the Spring 1999 (No.10) issue of The Armchair Aesthete
https://1drv.ms/b/s!AlDbHVZtizQh3g_sK-M0-_lvONEp

"The Bridge," the April 1999 (Vol.5 No.4) issue of Timber Creek Review https://1drv.ms/b/s!AlDbHVZtizQh3hoHHhmy yWXBr2ID

"Flight," the June 18, 1999 (No.2615) issue of Christian Courier, also accepted by The Banner

"Chimeras," the Summer 1999 (Vol.4 No.1) issue of Kimera: A Journal of Fine Writing, nominated for the 1999 Pushcart Prize, also accepted by Michigan Quarterly Review and Baltimore Review
http://www.js.spokane .wa.us/kimerav4n1/

zhang.htm

https://1drv.ms/b/s!AlDbHVZtizQh3hBwDcd4oKJNfuu5

"Defection," the September 1999 (Vol.19 No.2) issue of Words

of Wisdom https://1drv.ms/b/s!AlDbHVZtizQh3huX-LbWy4A--Dr9

"The Jaundice Ward," the Fall 1999 (Vol.4 No.1) issue of Five Points: A Journal of Literature & Arts

https://1drv.ms/b/s!AlDbHVZtizQh3hIN9F3uFobK4gm_

"Chicken Blood Therapy," the Winter 1999 (Vol.6 No.2) issue of Pangolin Papers, also nominated for the 1999 Pushcart Prize

https://1drv.ms/b/s!AlDbHVZtizQh3hhDawIEpEG4qP_o

Published as a reprint in the Spring 2000 (No.15) issue of The Edge City Review https://1drv.ms/b/s!AlDbHVZtizQhoCwUVexlRSL 09SKP

"Boomerang," the March 2000 (No. 18) issue of The Long Story

https://1drv.ms/b/s!AlDbHVZtizQhoC6GMzw Ta 0oi6KnL

"Inspection," the Winter 2001 (Vol.1 No.9) issue of Red Rock Review https://1drv.ms/b/s!AlDbHVZtizQh3h9hpvsUkvYR WQ83

"Trojan Rooster," the Fall 2002 (Nos. 55-56) issue of The Minnesota Review https://1drv.ms/b/s!AlDbHVZtizQh3hl1gfyeAHlG5WI_

《紫藤簃》(林本源家族训眉记纪事散文)
人民东方出版社 2017 英文书名：Wisteria Arbor

《五零后的回眸》上、下卷（自传散文集）
美国南方出版社 2018

Generation Mao: a Memoir Volume 1 & 2

Dixie W Publishing Corporation,

https://www.amazon.com/Generation-Mao-Memoir-1-Chinese/dp/1683721535

https://www.amazon.com/Generation-Mao-Memoir-2-Chinese/dp/1683721594

251

《半句多》美国南方出版社2019。

Speaking UP, Dixie W Publishing Corporation,

http://www.dwpcbooks.com/product/html/?241.html

《Expatriates》/《离乡人》美国南方出版社 2019。Dixie W Publishing Corporation,

http://www.dwpcbooks.com/product/html/?248.html

http://www.dwpcbooks.com/product/html/?252.html

Made in the USA
Lexington, KY
28 September 2019